Shesquatch Share
Card/Page

Title **Lily & Her Critter Friends**

Author **Sally W Eppstein**

The Awesome Owner

Date Borrowed		Date Returned
	MAC	
O	BERTIE	
	UWI	

Written and Illustrated

By

Sally Wansboro Eppstein

Copyright © 2022

Sally Wansboro Eppstein

Dedication

This book is dedicated to my husband, Jonathan Eppstein, who always supports my wild ideas.

To Maggie Eppstein, my sister-in-law, who helped me greatly.

Finally, to Peter Wansboro, my brother, for our own epic adventures section hiking the Appalachian Trail together.

May we have many more miles together.

All
The
Awesome
Characters

The Main Critter Posse

Lily
The Loving Shesquatch

Ruth
The Watchful Grandma Crow

Jojo
The Wicked Smart Blue Jay

Burfoot
The Super Eager Squirrel

Rory
The Worrisome Raccoon

The Main Critter Posse's
Foxes

Rusty
Protective Dad Fox

Rose
Super Chatty Fox

The Family

The Colonel
Super Dad

Judy
Amazing Mom

Hazel
Dot's Best Friend

The Furry Ones

Dot
Hazel's Best Friend

Boris
Mr. Grumpy

Other Characters

Jimbo
The Mean Moonshine Man

Betty
Red Bloodhound Pup

The Sheriff
A Kind Thoughtful Man

Peter
The Hometown Deputy

Beverly
The Bashful Beaver

Special Guest

Baldy
The Bald Eagle

Remi
The Red Tail Hawk

Olly

Opal
The Opossum

Benny
The Black Bear

The Scurriers

Squirrels

Burfoot   Jermey

The Super Eager Squirrel   **The Reliable Caboose**

Chipmunks

Both Day & Night Critters

The Radical Raccoon Family

Rory
Again

Brothers

Morgan
Dad

Morgan's Kids

Abby

MORGAN Jr.

The Night Crew

Trio of Mighty Owls

Ester
The
Screech Owl

Barney
The
Barred Owl

Gretchen
The
Great Horned
Owl

The Broadcasters Barn Owls

The Night Crew
Continued

Gilded Gliders

30 Flying Squirrels

FunK the SkunK

The Red Hot Headbangers

Pearl
The Pileated Woodpecker

The Mighty Downy Woodpecker

Red
The Redheaded
Woodpecker

Contents

1 * Dot a Black and White Dog * Getting Lost

"Dot, stop! Come back! You are going to get lost.", screamed Hazel.

Dot had been hiking with Hazel, her human sister, and the Colonel, her human dad, on the Appalachian Trail when she saw the most majestic creatures running through the forest. Dot got so excited she twisted and turned until she slipped out of her collar and began running full bore to follow a herd of deer, leaving Hazel and the Colonel behind. The group ran together, jumping over creeks, rocks, and fallen trees. They climbed steep hills and dashed into deep valleys until they reached a wide river. Dot was in such a trance; she didn't hear a word; the family shouted at her to stop and come back.

After running for miles, Dot crawled into the river's shallows, lapping the chilly water to cool her body down. Then she found a nice sunny spot on the water's edge and rolled on her back, letting the sun warm her belly as she wiggled to get the excess water off her back.

Once she had caught her breath and was warmed by the sun, she chased the fawns around the trees as the rest of the herd drank, ate acorns, and leafy greens.

As the daylight dimmed, Dot's eyes suddenly widened, and she gulped, "My family, where are they?" With worried eyes, Dot looked at the leader of the herd.

1

He grunted, "Stay put tonight, so you stay safe." She was surprised she understood him. She nodded her head but reluctantly sat down. Dot then raised her nose, inhaling deeply to see if she could catch the scent of her human family.

2 * The Humans *
Heartbroken

What Dot didn't know was that her family was worried sick about her. They hollered her name until they were hoarse, as well as asking all the hikers on the trail if they had seen their small black and white puppy. Unfortunately, everyone said no. As the sun went down, they had no choice but to go home and devise a game plan to find Dot the next day. Ten-year-old Hazel cried all the way home and her dad, the Colonel, gripped the steering wheel tightly in utter sadness, knowing he would have to tell his wife and Hazel's younger sisters, the twins, that Dot was missing. What the humans did not know was that there were many eyes on Dot.

3 * The Critters *
Always Watching

Ruth, a wise and observant older crow, had been watching Dot from afar when the puppy suddenly and recklessly ran away from her family. Ruth had also seen how Hazel and the Colonel panicked as they witnessed Dot and the herd of whitetail deer disappearing through the maze of trees. She felt her heart break, she was close to her large family. Ruth knew she had to do something about this situation quickly.

As soon as Dot had bolted, Ruth let out a loud call to gather her murder of crows. They rapidly flocked to her, landing on the swaying branches of a large silver maple with a few leaves still hanging. Each crow gave Ruth their undivided attention.

She announced, "There is a young pup we must help right away. She will never survive the bone-chilling temperatures coming our way. We must tell Lily so she can round up both the day and night troops, and we can create a plan to bring this family back together. From now on, all future meetings and updates will be at Lily's Den."

She ordered ten crows to follow the dog with the herd of deer, and another ten crows were directed to follow the humans. Then Ruth called William, the fastest-flying crow of the murder. Ruth cackled to William, "Go, as fast as you can tell Lily; we need to think about food, a day crew, a night crew, and how to get this dog home before the temperatures dip below freezing in the next few days." She cawed loudly to all, "Go!" and the group of crows lifted from the tree in a large iridescent black mass that quickly broke apart, flying off on their new mission.

4 * Lily's Den *
The Command Center

Lily, a female Bigfoot, was the mastermind of her territory in the forest. She stood seven feet tall and was covered with shaggy brown hair with furry feet and hands. Lily referred to herself as a Shesquatch, instead of a Bigfoot or Sasquatch. She was very secretive with humans, but most birds and animals were her friends. Her primary goal was to help as many critters and humans as possible when needed. She led a vast network of woodland comrades who loved to assist her.

Swiftly flying down, William blurted out, "We have a new emergency, a lost dog!" as he tried to land on the moss-covered bolder, guarding the entrance to Lily's den, but he stumbled, tripped, falling off the large rock. He flapped his wings wildly to get control, then flew up to land where he meant to the first time. He was incredibly fast but awfully clumsy. "It is a short-haired pup, so it will not do well with the cold, and the family is worried sick. Groups of crows are following both the pup and the family."

Trying to maintain a straight face due to William's landing, she paused until she knew she wouldn't laugh, she expressed, "I am so glad the crows are tracking both groups, but the poor little puppy and family must be worried sick. Here we go, a new mission!"

She then let out a loud whistle to call her neighbor, Rusty, a red fox, as she climbed out of her den.

Rusty bolted out of his rooted den, located under an ancient tulip poplar tree as soon as he heard her call. He ran the short distance to meet Lily. Together they slipped through the dense forest to a unique hollow tree. She took a large stick and hit the tree three times, creating a booming noise that resonated for miles through the woods. Rusty followed with a loud, piercing scream. This was the "alarm call" for her troop to come to Lily's den, the command center, figure out how to help whoever was in need.

Two crews started to report to the command center. The wide-awake day crew was first to arrive.

Jojo flew into Lily's den. He was a large blue jay who, without exception, seemed to have a musical beat going on in his head so he was constantly swaying, bopping, and bouncing up and down. He never seemed to be paying attention. However, Jojo was wicked smart. He handled logistics for each rescue mission and managed the critters' wide-ranging skill sets. He was Lily's right-hand man or bird, you could say.

"Hey, Lil. It's good to be on a mission again; I've been a bit bored." Jojo stated while bobbing his head.

Next was Rory, the loyal, anxious, and easily frightened raccoon. He was always thinking about the worst-case scenario, which helped keep him extra alert and on his toes.

"What now? Is it bad? Did someone break a leg?" Rory asked as his mind went a mile a minute pondering all the bad things that could go wrong in the woods.

Rusty, the fox, who had the loudest scream in the forest, but was never one for conversation, had just returned with his daughter, Rose. Unlike her dad, she loved to bark and squeal non-stop.

Rose started with her usual excited chatter, "Hey y'all, how is everyone doing? It is so good to see everyone again!" but when she glanced at her dad, she knew to stop. Rusty liked Rose to be quiet when a new mission was about to be discussed and plans developed.

Next, the gang of woodpeckers, known as the 'Red Hot Headbangers,' flew in. They loved filling the forest with their magical beat.

The leader of the 'Headbangers', is Pearl, a pileated woodpecker, the largest woodpecker in the woods. She was so proud of her large crown of red feathers.

The rest of the gang included her five friends, the downy woodpeckers, the smallest woodpeckers who are incredibly brave and hard working.

The last of the Headbangers to join in was Red, the very special red-headed woodpecker, who loved the thrill of catching insects in flight and hiding his food in different trees. He considered himself a great warrior.

Joining together the Headbangers flew up and synchronized their formation in flight to circle Lily's den, then they landed on the surrounding trees. Altogether, they started hammering the trees in a low rhythmic beat.

"Caw." Ruth greeted everyone, including a few of her crow family who were not on the mission already.

Bouncing, running, and tumbling like a furry whirlwind, making a huge racket in the dry leaves, rolled in the 'Scurriers,' a big crew of squirrels and chipmunks.

"The day crew is all here!" Jojo announced proudly.

Lily smiled and nodded to him.

Slowly but surely, the night crew, still a bit groggy since they had all just woken up, came to Lily's den.

They included the 'Gilded Gliders,' a troop of thirty flying squirrels.

The famous 'Trio' of mighty owls, Barney, the barred owl, Gretchen, the great horned owl, and Ester, the eastern screech owl glided in.

Ester took over Jojo's job in the when the sun was down. She, too, was wicked smart, but her personality was the polar opposite of Jojo's. She was seriously prim and proper and proudly held her beak high.

"Evening Lily and everyone else. I am so happy to see you all again." Ester turned her head to make eye contact with everyone, just as her mother taught her.

In addition to the power trio, flew in the Broadcasters, a tight-knit parliament of twelve barn owls who took over the communication from the daytime crows.

Last to join the diverse group, but definitely not the least, Funk, the skunk, who had one of the most awesome mighty powers of all. "I am ready to get my spray on." Funk laughed at his patented joke he predictably said at the

7

beginning of each mission.

While this impressive team was assembled for the kick-off meeting at the command center, there were hundreds of other forest critters ready to spring into action if needed.

"I hope this is an easy mission to reunite this young puppy with his family. I'm grateful to have all of you here", Lily told the crowd.

5 * The Humans *
Dinnertime

As the family sat down for dinner, a fog of grief and fear settled over the whole family. They pushed the chicken, green peas, and stewed apples around on their plates, taking only a few bites here and there. The two-year-old twins, who loved to play with their food and usually ate every morsel, including the green peas, ate only a fraction.

Even the always hungry, grumpy, orange, and white tabby cat, Boris, who never failed to beg for table scraps, was sad and worried. On this evening, he, too, didn't have the energy to beg. Boris had been very jealous of Dot for showing up six months ago because now, Boris got fewer food scraps and less attention from his humans. He would show his discontent by flicking his tail wildly, while giving Dot the death stare. Shocked by his own sadness about Dot being lost, Boris left the dining room to sit at his

8

favorite spot on the table looking out the front bay window. His tail hung heavily off the table, but he was watching everything that moved outside, hoping Dot would show up.

After dinner and late into the night, the Colonel and Hazel printed out hundreds of "Lost Dog" flyers announcing a big reward of $1,500 with pictures of Dot, their phone number, address.

6 * Dot and The Herd of Deer * Bedtime

As darkness slipped over the forest, the stars started popping out, one by one, in the blackish blue sky. Dot went around the camp for the last time trying to figure out which direction she came from, while noticing her belly was starting to rumble. She was hungry, cold, scared, and sad. At home, she always slept with her human sister in the cozy, warm bed that smelled of fresh soap with a full belly. She thought about the yummy leftovers, her canned dog food, and the sausage-like treats her family gave her. With a heavy heart and empty stomach, Dot laid down and tried to get comfortable. She curled up next to her new friend, a six-month-old spotted fawn on a nest of fragrant pine needles. While the pine needles smelled nice, it wasn't the same as Hazel's bed. She let out a sad whimper as she finally rested her head on the fawn's neck. Dot's eyelids were getting heavy, and she started to fall asleep, but she was startled awake by the yipping and howls of a large pack of coyotes. Unable to keep her eyes open, they fluttered closed, but her ears were cocked back in fearful alertness.

7 * The Humans *
Bedtime

After Hazel said good night to her family, she crawled into her bed and the intensity of her grief expanded in her broken heart. She and Dot had a nightly routine. Each night, they played hide and seek from each other, over and under the covers they tried to hide, until they were worn out. Then Dot would get under the covers, dig with her paws as she went in circles multiple times until it was just perfect, and then she would curl up next to Hazel. They would both fall asleep, keeping each other warm and feeling secure.

Laying down on an empty bed, Hazel was overwhelmed by grief. She smushed her face into her pillow and cried. Boris the cat, who hated to share a bed with Dot, softly jumped up on the bed. He rested his big furry body next to Hazel's head and put a large paw on her shoulder as Hazel slipped into dreamland.

What the humans didn't know was that Barney, the watchful barred owl, a squad of barn owls, and the sleeping crew of daytime crows, were all stationed outside of Hazel's house. They were taking turns keeping a watchful eye over

Hazel, the entire home, and the surrounding neighborhood, both day and night.

8 * The Command Center * Daybreak

As the morning sun started to peek over the hills and through the trees, all members of both the day and night crews, except for those assigned to watching the house, met again at Lily's den.

Lily whistled to get everyone's attention. "Okay, the plan is simple, all we need to do is to reunite Dot with her family when they come back to the trail, as the family said yesterday."

Lily assigned Rusty and Rose, the father-daughter fox team, along with ten squirrels, and five crows, telling them to go to the trailhead parking lot next to downtown to keep an eye out for the humans.

"When the family leaves their house, the crows stationed there will update us with their progress towards the trailhead", said Lily.

Next, Lily looked at Jojo, who was dancing to the music in his head." Jojo, are you paying attention?" Jojo kept bopping and nodding his head to his inner beat but focused his full attention on Lily. She winked at him signaling that she knew she had his attention. "All right, everyone, the timing needs to be perfect, so Dot and the humans can meet on the path at the same time."

The Red Hot Headbangers were starting their rhythmic beat on the surrounding trees in anticipation of the day's reunion.

Jojo started bobbing up and down while flapping his wings, getting pumped up and ready for the mission to begin.

But then there was Rory, the worrisome raccoon. He was anxiously peppering Lily with questions about how things could go sideways. "Lily, what if we don't get them together? What if the coyotes come around? What if Dot doesn't want to follow the group? Should we get Sasquatch?"

Lily loved Rory, but his questions and worries took up so much time. She looked at him and said "Rory, it will be okay, if a problem arrives, we will adapt and bend like a willow tree in the wind. Let's just trust everything will work out. The rest of you please standby for updates and any changes in our plans."

Adrenalin was high and all the critters were bursting from head to toe with excitement, ready to get Dot reunited with her family.

9 * The Humans *
Breakfast

The family was up eating breakfast, or we should say, trying to eat breakfast. They had scrambled eggs and toast, but they were still in the fog of sadness with little appetite. After breakfast, the Colonel and Hazel made PB&J and baloney sandwiches for their lunch and dinner for their upcoming day trip back on the trail to search for Dot. Plus, they made sure to pack Dot's favorite dog treats, water, and a bowl, putting it all in the Colonel's bright orange backpack.

Boris was looking out the window, when he noticed the crows and owls perched on the big, old, oak tree in the front yard. "Strange.", Boris thought.

Barney, the barred owl, turned his head to stare directly into Boris's eyes, a very long stare. Boris, frightened, stood up, arched his back, and subconsciously spiked his fur. As he studied the owl, his posture started to relax, and he started to get a good feeling.

When Barney saw Boris relax, he nodded his head, and blinked his large, dark, eyes, reassuringly. Boris flicked the tip of his tail in understanding. He felt the start of a strange friendship being formed between himself and the owl.

The Colonel and Hazel gathered the flyers that they were going to post around their quaint downtown. Then they would hit the trail to start their search for Dot, in the dense forest.

The mom and twins shouted, "Goodbye and we hope you find her!", as the two left the house.

While driving towards downtown, both Hazel and the Colonel noticed a handful of crows who appeared to be following them. They both pointed and laughed at what they thought was a strange coincidence. It was not a fluke, they were being followed, while other crows continued to keep an attentive eyes on their home.

10 * The Deer Herd *
Morning

Dot was waking up to a misty, chilly morning, when a large crow poked its beak into Dot's face. Dot jumped with surprise, looking directly into Ruth's eyes. Ruth then gave a loud caw to Jojo to let him know that Dot was awake.

Jojo let out five quick calls, to signal to the bald eagle, to drop the freshly caught trout for Dot's breakfast.

Dot was still trying to figure out why this strange blackbird was hopping around, when the eagle dropped the trout about an inch from her black snout. She jumped back, startled yet again. She looked over to the herd of deer, scared, and confused, but they all seemed to have a smile glistening in their eyes, as they ate. Ruth hopped to Dot, then hopped back to the freshly killed trout, over and over, until Dot got the message. Dot slowly went to the trout to smell it. The aroma made her drool, and then she remembered how hungry she was. Dot didn't need not be told again; she started eating right away.

11 * The Humans *
Setting out Flyers

Hazel and the Colonel got out of their car and started putting flyers on the telephone poles along Main Street. They entered the stores and asked to put flyers on the doors, and everyone kindly agreed. They took the remaining flyers and put them on the cars in the parking lot between the drug store and the approach trail. Everyone in town was compassionately eager to be on the lookout for the lost puppy.

12 * The Mean Moonshine Man *

Jimbo, short for Jimmy Johnson, was a tall, skinny, crusty, old, moonshine man who didn't much like anyone including himself. Although, sometimes he showed a little bit of affection for his bloodhound, Betty, who was so skinny most of her ribs showed. Betty was in the bed of the beat-up, rusty-red, old truck and Jimbo sat in the warm cab at a stop sign on Main Street. Jimbo watch the father and daughter get out of their fancy sedan. "Oooh-wee, look at that uppity automobile, they sure do look like they got themselves a whole bunch of money".

Then Jimbo noticed they were putting up flyers, he decided to pull over to park so he could see what they were up to. As soon as they entered the drug store, he jumped out of his truck, snatching one of the flyers from a telephone pole. He started laughing and said, "Betty, we got us a new plan today! We goin' to find that, there, dog and claim a big,ole ree-ward. Hee-hee-hee." He cackled followed by a ragged cough; he started his truck which didn't sound much better than he did.

13 * Dot and the other Critters * On the Move

After Dot was done eating, Ruth nodded to Jojo, up in the branches. Jojo let out a cry to alert the crew that they were about to move. The squirrels scampered down from the trees, ready to lead the way. First, Ruth needed to get Dot, pointed in the right direction. Ruth stretched out her wings and circled behind Dot, flapping her wings until Dot was pointed east, heading back towards the Appalachian Trail.

As soon as Burfoot, an overly excited squirrel, saw Dot was pointed in the right direction she took off running without waiting for her que from Jojo. Dot's eyes nearly popped out of her head. She barked "Squirrel!" and took off in fast pursuit, to everyone's surprise, especially Burfoot's, Dot was catching up fast and nipping at

Burfoot's tail. Burfoot didn't take too kindly to Dot chasing her at all. She stopped abruptly and nimbly stepped aside so Dot didn't run her over. Dot tried to stop, turned to look for Burfoot, but lost her footing, and became a blur of black and white that rolled right into a big maple tree. Dot was dazed, shaken up, and pawed her head where she hit the tree. Then Burfoot marched right over to Dot, stood on her hind legs, and chirped loudly while pointing her little finger and said, "Oh no missy. You have no right to try to eat me. I'm here to help you. If you eat me up, I can tell you right now that none of the other squirrels or chipmunks will be willing to help you at all. Do you understand me?" All the other Scurriers murmured in agreement as they nodded their heads in unison.

Jojo and Ruth flew down next to Dot to back up Burfoot. Ruth said, "Okay, we are here to help you. Our goal is to get you back with your family who will be out on the trail looking for you today. You are to follow the squirrels, raccoons, birds or whoever we tell you to follow but you are not allowed to eat any of them. Do you understand?"

Dot's head lifted at the thought of being back with her family and she let out a grateful yelp.

Jojo looked at Burfoot and said, "Wait for me to give the orders." Burfoot was filled with so much excitement she nodded her head but didn't hear a word he said. Jojo gave the squirrels the command to carry on and told William to give Lily the update. The squirrels and Dot took off, followed above by Jojo, Ruth, and a few of her clan, darting through the treetops as they kept an eye on the convoy.

17

14 * The Mean Moonshine Man * Looking for A Scent

Jimbo drove to Dot's house and circled the block three times to get a feel for the neighborhood. He parked his truck around the corner from the house, got Betty out of the bed of the truck, and put her leash on. As they started walking, he let Betty take her time to stop and smell everything. He wanted to eyeball all the surroundings while scheming how he and Betty could find Dot before anyone else.

Once he reached Dot's house, he saw dog toys in the front yard. Seeing the toys gave him an exciting tingling that spread from his crusty toes to the top of his thinning gray-hair. He looked about to make sure no one was around. What he didn't realize was Boris, the big orange cat, had been watching him and Betty's every move. The second Jimbo stepped on the family's lawn, Boris let out a very loud alarm meow hoping to get the attention of Hazel's mom, Judy. Boris wanted her to see what the strange man was up to.

To shake off the sadness from one of their family members missing, Judy decided to distract herself and the twins with a singing and dancing show on the TV in the backroom. Because the volume was so loud, they didn't hear Boris. However, the crows did hear Boris and had been watching the tall skinny man all along. They cawed to wake Barney, the barred owl. His eyes popped open, blinking slowly a few times, then turning his head to focus on the man. He flapped his wings to awaken the barn owls so they, too, could get a visual of this man and his dog. The Broadcasters turned their heads to witness the skinny man' behavior.

They all watched as Jimbo tiptoed across the yard, around Hazel's and the twin's toys, to get to a red rubber ball and a monkey toy with rope legs and arms. He grabbed both dog toys, stuffed them into his canvas coat pockets, turned, and quickly got back on the sidewalk, looking out to make sure no one had seen him. Boris let out a second piercing yowl, again trying to alert Judy. However, the loud singing was still going on, rendering mute his yowl for help. Boris rolled his eyes and then looked up to the birds. Barney, the crows, the Broadcasters, and Boris all made eye contact with the feline. They stared at each other confirming that they had all witnessed an evil act since they each had a spidey-sense something bad was going down.

Barney told one of the crows to inform Lily and the rest of the critters what they had just witnessed. Although, they were a bit confused about what the scraggly man with the bloodhound dog's intentions were.

A crow flew off to give Lily the message. A few other crows began to fly from tree to tree, following the man. Boris gave his new friend, Barney, a sly smile as he flicked his tail, in encouragement, and hopeful anticipation. Barney nodded his head to Boris and then dozed off to get his beauty sleep, leaving the rest of the crows on the lookout as the owls rested for their night shift.

When Jimbo got around the corner, close to his rusty, old, truck, he pulled out the toys and told Betty, "Smell girl." Young, kind-hearted Betty inhaled the distinctive smell of Dot and pranced on all four paws in excitement. The crows soared overhead as the two got in the truck and followed Jimbo as he drove towards downtown.

15 * Command Center *
Mid-Morning

The crows came in from all locations to update Lily and Rory about Dot, the family, and this strange new man in the red truck.

As was his nature, worrisome Rory started to panic, "Who is this man in the red truck? Why is he laughing and stealing toys? Oh, I just don't like this. No, no, no. Not one bit! Oh dear, oh dear, oh dear. Bug smasher. This was supposed to be easy. Is he a good man? A Bad man? A really really bad man? I think he is bad. Bad, bad, bad. Yep, that is what I think." Rory sputtered out.

Lily tried to calm Rory down. "Rory, you're worried about nothing, it is just some man. We've got to hope for the best and trust that Dot and her family will be reunited."

Rory just looked at her blankly, twitched his long white whiskers, and then slowly reached to give them a long slow pull. Rory decided to find something to eat to help settle his nerves.

Lily shook off Rory's unease and looked at the reporting crows." Thanks so much for the updates. We hope to get Dot and her family back together no later than this afternoon. Please continue keep us apprised of what's going on."

At that, the crows flapped their wings and headed back to their different observation posts.

16 * The Humans *
Mid-Morning Break

After handing out and stapling flyers for a couple of hours, the Colonel and Hazel sat down on the bench behind the drug store, by the parking lot leading to the entry to the Appalachian Trail. The Colonel was drinking coffee and Hazel was drinking hot cocoa to warm-up before they hit the trail to look for Dot.

Hazel let out a long sigh while attempting to bite into a massive dob of whipped cream piled high on top of her steaming cup, "Dad, I am so scared we are not going to find Dot. All I can think about is her being alone in the woods, being hungry, cold, and scared. I miss her so much; she is my best friend." Hazel paused before she continued, "I am so scared I won't ever see her again." Letting out an even longer sigh she then dropped her head on her dad's arm.

The Colonel understood only too well how Hazel was feeling. Dot was a Father's Day gift for him and, even though Hazel and Dot were inseparable, the Colonel had his own special relationship with Dot. He loved when Dot cuddled up on his lap while he watched the evening news, how she magically appeared in the kitchen when he was making his sandwiches for lunch, or the way she ripped around the backyard running so fast with a huge smile on her face like she was possessed with a happy spirit. Her energy brings so much joy to this family.

The Colonel could only respond with his own deep sigh and hugged her closely. They went silent as the vintage steam locomotive full of tourists was approaching the parking lot. They first heard the train's bell, followed by the loud steam whistle, and knew it was fruitless to try to talk. They waved to the passengers who waved to them. After the caboose passed, the hikers and backpackers crossed over the tracks to go north on the trail or south into the parking lot. They saw an old pickup truck with the words "Firewood for sale" painted on the side, but the "r and the s" were printed backwards. Driving the truck was the mean moonshine man with Betty was sitting in the back with firewood and boxes of glass jars of full of illegal moonshine covered by a tarp.

Betty looked at Hazel and let out a friendly yowl as she picked up the scent of Dot coming from the young family. Jimbo noticed the family and freaked out a little bit because he didn't want to attract any attention. He yelled to Betty, "Shut up girl!", as he pulled away leaving a noxious plume of black exhaust in their wake.

Hazel and her dad just looked at each other as they fanned the stink away, then the Colonel tapped Hazel's knee and said," Okay, let's do it. Let's find our girl." They walked through the parking lot onto the Appalachian Trail, carrying Dot's favorite treats and the yummy baloney, her truly favorite sandwich meat.

17 * The Mean Moonshine Man *
A Delay

Jimbo was delighted, because he and Betty got back downtown in no time, since the family lived so close. After finding the dog's toys he was planning on hitting the trail immediately, before he made his deliveries of firewood and moonshine. When he heard Betty baying out a loud howl, Jimbo got excited because he thought she had gotten a scent of Dot. But then he looked around and spotted the little girl and her dad. He then figured out that they were the source of the scent that triggered Betty's sounding off. His heart gave an extra beat and he almost panicked, but he stayed cool.

"Cheeseburgers!", Jimbo cursed under his breath, frustrated, he knew he would be competing with the family for who would find the dog first. Jimbo decided to leave but had a second heart-pounding moment when the town sheriff eased up next to his truck and waved him to stop. He was trying real hard to be cool while his hands and legs were shaking with fright. He had three boxes full of illegal moonshine in the back of this truck. Jimbo smiled as big as he could and said, "Howdy Sheriff, how you doing today? It's a fine day ain't it? Ain't these blue skies something? I hear there is a bit of cold weather coming our way." Then he yelled to

himself in his head, "Shut up, shut up, shut up!".
He always talked too much when he was
nervous.

The Sheriff just laughed, replying, "Why
yes, it is a wonderful day. I just wanted to talk to
you about that good lookin' hound dog you've
got."

Jimbo was thinking fast, panicking that the
sheriff was going to get out of his car and find the
homemade brew. Jimbo, again, started talking a
mile a minute. "Well sir, she is a fine youngin,
just a year old next month. Her granddaddy was
a national champ, but I got her for real cheap
because no one wanted her 'cause she was such
a tiny little runt, but she done growed up just fine,
see how big she is? She is my favorite color, red.
I recon all them other colors of bloodhounds are
just fine but for me, red's the best. My family has
always had red bloodhounds, so I just like to
keep the tradition up, you know?"

The sheriff laughed again, "Oh I know, our
family tradition is plott hounds; I have always
wanted a bloodhound, but my papa never let me
get one." Ready to leave as quickly as he could,
Jimbo told the sheriff, "Well if you ever need to
borrow my girl Betty here to find a scent you just
let me know, you hear?"

The sheriff nodded, tipped his hat, and
said, "Thanks so much, I'll definitely keep that in
mind. What's your name?"
"Jimmy Johnson, sir but everyone calls me
Jimbo, I sell firewood, sir." Jimbo tipped his own
hat and eased out of the parking lot trailed by a
large cloud of black exhaust that made Betty
sneeze loudly, then she braced herself against
the truck's acceleration. The faster they went the
bigger the chill. She gave herself a big shake as if

to shake away the cold and the dirty exhaust with her huge ears flapping wildly. Then she crawled underneath the tarp with the moonshine and laid down as they picked up speed.

As Jimbo drove away, he thought about what a fool he was to offer Betty for any kind of service to the sheriff. He was proud that he had lived in this town all his life and only a few folks really knew who he was, what he did, and where he lived. He loved being a loner because people for some strange reason always made him mad and that's why some folks gave him his other nickname, "the mean moonshine man". This nickname made him a bit sad, but then he just got mad some more, and then he got spiteful. It was a vicious cycle of being sad, then mad, then even madder.

18 * The Critters *
Command Center Updates

The crows had been flying back and forth updating Rory, Ruth, and Lily. Lily was taking freshly fallen leaves down to her den to get ready for the first freeze, coming their way soon. Ruth was happy to be back on her favorite perch to let Jojo and all the other critters do more of the work today, as she was ready for a nap. Rory, on the other hand, was easily distracted diving into piles of leaves that Lily had made, rolling around, doing somersaults, and wiggling on his back listening to the leaves giggle.

Lily rolled her eyes and smiled; these are the things in life that give her the greatest joy. She was also happy because Dot and her family were going to be reunited today.

The humans were on the trail heading their way while Burfoot and the other squirrels were heading back to the spot where Dot and her family had separated the day before. The man in the truck was off doing something else. Everything was going just perfectly.

19 * Dot and the Critters *
Mid-Morning

Burfoot and the others were moving at a fast clip as she led the group to her favorite moss-covered log to cross the wide creek with its rapid water. She was a bit shocked when she got to the creek and saw that the log was gone. Standing up on her hind legs she looked around and directed the other squirrels to look for the crossing log. Jojo was also looking, flying up and down the creek. Then he announced that the log was gone, and everyone agreed it must have been washed away in the last storm.

Jojo and Burfoot walked away from the others to figure out a new plan for crossing the creek, while one of the crows went to update the command center, telling them they had hit a snag.

Jojo said to Burfoot, "The best place to cross this creek without a log is about 20 miles north of here." Burfoot shook her head and said, "Oh no, that will not do, that would take way too much time."

Then Burfoot suggested, "We could just throw Dot in the water and tell her to swim fast to the other side."

Jojo shook his head and said, "Too cold."

Burfoot continued, "We can get the bald eagle to carry her over the creek."

Jojo shook his head a second time, "I would be worried the eagle's talons would hurt Dot."

Out of the corner of Jojo's eye, he saw a movement. He hopped over to try to see what it was, but whatever he saw moved. Burfoot ran over to the large group of old trees to try to see what Jojo had seen. As they circled the trees, the mysterious black shadow was just one step ahead of them. Jojo jumped up to fly in the opposite direction from Burfoot and he let out an accusing cry, "I gotcha!"

A big fat beaver froze, covered her eyes, then fell over on her side in fright. Jojo flew down and screamed, "Perfect!"

Beverly, the beaver, removed one paw from her left eye and stuttered, "Wh wh wh what?"

Jojo yelled at Burfoot, "Come quick, I have the perfect solution to our problem!"

Seeing the beaver, Burfoot did her happy dance bouncing up and down and whipping her tail side to side, while letting out happy chirps.

"Quick, follow me, quick!", Jojo ordered the beaver, not noticing Beverly's extreme discomfort as she trailed behind the pair with reluctance. They all reached the water's edge and Jojo announced," We need you to cut down a

27

tree big enough for our friend Dot to cross the creek, will you help us?" Beverly slowly looked around at all the critters, including Dot, who was panting with a happy smile. The shy beaver was silently freaking out at all the attention from everyone watching her with wide eyes and nodding heads.

Beverly stuttered again, "Wh wh wh what?", even though she understood what they wanted, but she was stalling for time to process all the things happening so quickly in her normally tranquil life.

Jojo was getting impatient so he broke out into a rap, to hopefully get Beverly motivated and moving.

*"**This here is Dot**
Dot got lost.
You can help cut down a tree, don't you know.
You can be a hero.
Dot loves her humans.
So it would be a beautiful reunion."*

Jojo landed on Beverly's head, did a few twirls, then brought one of his eyes to one of her eyes and questioned, "See?".

Beverly fainted. Jojo flew up so he wouldn't get crushed, while all the other critters just stared in disbelief for a moment. Quickly, all the squirrels ran to Beverly, each grabbing a leaf, and started fanning her like crazy.

Beverly woke up, stared at all the squirrels so close to her, she jumped up, and ran away. This was way too much for her to handle. All the critters were crestfallen. Jojo used his wing in a movement to tell all the critters to hide, except for Dot and Burfoot.

Burfoot ran up to Beverly softly said "Oh please help us, I am so sorry about Jojo and his bad little rap. Normally he is super chill but sometimes he gets over-excited and breaks out in song and dance. It is his only bad quality."

Beverly just stared at Burfoot with skeptical eyes. Dot walked up hesitantly, laid down next to Beverly, and said, "Please help me, it is getting colder, and I just don't have much fur to keep me warm, like you do. I can't hibernate like a bear. I don't have feathers I can fluff out. I don't have a have a bunch of siblings to snuggle up with at night. Can you please, please, pleeease help me?"

Dot then gave Beverly her best food-begging eyes that she had been practicing for months with her humans.

Finally, Beverly turned around, looked at Burfoot, and said, "Whi whi which tree?"

"I have the perfect tulip poplar tree. Follow me.", Burfoot said. Beverly nodded her head, approached the tree, and got to work. Everyone around her stayed silent, so they wouldn't scare Beverly again.

Jojo nodded to a crow to update Lily at the command center about what was going on. The squirrels hung out in the branches of the trees, watching Beverly work. Dot laid down and Burfoot crawled on top of Dot, so they both could have a bit more warmth while they watched the chips fly from Beverly's sharp incisors.

The Red Hot Headbangers came to watch when they heard about Beverly's contribution to the rescue operation. They wanted to see the action and to give some musical encouragement. They started a soft, yet fast, rhythmic beat on the surrounding trees.

Jojo bobbed his head and all the other critters got into the groove, too. Even Beverly caught the beat.

With the beat driving her, the chips flew even faster. The tree started to rock back and forth, as the wind was getting stronger, but the breeze was blowing the tree in the wrong direction! The tree started to lean towards the forest instead of the creek. All the critters were watching in suspense. Jojo pointed his wing to the tree, directing all the squirrels to leap onto the bare branches on the creek side of the tulip poplar to pull the tree back towards the creek, wrestling against the wind. Some were jumping on the branches and some squirrels were pulling with their arms as they pumped their hanging bodies and fluffy tails. Slowly, the tree started bending towards the creek, but the wind picked up and started to push it towards the forest again. All the crows jumped on the branches flapping their wings to help. As the tree began arching again over creek, Beverly worked even faster, and the tree was getting close to falling. The Red Hot Headbangers jumped on the tree and when the tree was over the creek, they would all start hammering as hard and fast as they could.

Dot couldn't just stand by to watch, so she ran up along the trunk of the bowing tree. Her additional weight was just enough to cause the tree to snap and to fall across the creek. As the tree fell, the crows and woodpeckers flew up, the squirrels leaped to nearby branches, Dot tumbled and rolled when she hit the ground, and they all let out a loud cheer, surrounding Beverly. She put her paws over her ears and tightly closed her eyes, not wanting to be a part of this loud celebration. When they realized they were scaring Beverly again, all the critters stopped in mid-celebratory cheer and quietly pretended to just go about their normal business.

Dot went slowly up to Beverly, until she was nose-to-nose to stare her into her eyes. Then Dot simply said, "Thank you so much." Beverly's eyes became moist with the warmth of sweet pride, and she said, "Yo yo you are welcome." and then she vanished into her safe haven of the old-growth trees.

20 * The Humans *
Back on the Trail

Hazel and her dad started trekking along the trail, trying to be positive and hoping they would find Dot quickly. They were grateful the sky was blue, and for the warmth of the sun shining through the nearly leafless trees.

Rusty, the red fox, Rose, his daughter, the squirrels, and the crows were following the two humans, keeping just off the trail so they would not be spotted. Rusty looked at Rose with his golden eyes to let Rose know she needed to be quiet. He knew it would be very hard for her because she loves to hear herself chatter. Rose got bored easily, and since she couldn't chat, she needed to do something to keep herself entertained. At different times Rose would stop for a bit, roll around, smell the different mushrooms, chew on sticks, or play with a willing squirrel or chipmunk. After trying to entertain herself, she would run back to her dad and the rest of the crew. This irritated Rusty, but he knew it was better than her non-stop chatter.

Hazel and the Colonel both looked deep into the woods, trying to spot Dot, and asking each hiker they passed if they had seen a small black and white dog. Unfortunately, the answer was always "No." When they were not talking to other hikers they continued calling out for Dot, taking turns to preserve their voices.

Rusty was also looking for the crows to alert him if Dot was close by. It was a truly joint mission, although the humans were completely unaware of all the woodland critters that were working to reunite Dot with her family.

21 * The Mean Moonshine Man *
Out Making Deliveries

After being startled by the sheriff, Jimbo decided to deliver his firewood and moonshine, then come back later to look for Dot. He was hoping to find her first.

Jimbo was traveling up a steep, thin, dirt road when two boys on an ATV flew down the hill heading right towards him. He jerked his truck hard to the right, hitting the brakes, and came to a jolting stop. He was relieved that he didn't hit the big oak tree next to the road. The boys continued past, hooting, and hollering as they drove away, unaware of running the truck off the road. Jimbo got out of his old pickup, mad as a swarm of hornets. Betty was pawing her head where she had a small cut from the shattered moonshine jars. Jimbo looked in the back of his truck, and the smell of all the moonshine hit him. Then he saw the blood on Betty's head and told her to get out of the truck. She walked nimbly around the river of moonshine streaming down the bed of the pickup. Jimbo removed the canvas tarp only to see every single one of his jars broken, and his firewood was now all wet.

He yelled down the hill, "Cheese and crackers! You stupid boys, if I ever see you again, I am going find your granny and tell her to put y'all in church with a pew full of sinners!"

He called for Betty to jump in the cab so he could turn around and run those boys down to teach them a lesson. He cranked up his truck, tried to start to drive, but realized something was wrong. The moonshine man got out of the truck and walked to the front passenger side where he saw his front tire was flat from hitting the roots of the old oak tree. He was so mad you could almost see the steam coming out of his ears! He started screaming every food he could think of, "Dill pickles! Hamburgers, pasta, egg yolks, ham hocks, darn tooting cheese grits!". He yelled so loud, scaring poor Betty who was trying to crawl under the front seat, but only her head would fit.

He grabbed his soaking wet, bald spare tire, tire-iron, and rusty old jack. Cussing up a storm, he started fretting about how he was going to change the tire on a hill.

22 * Command Center *
Getting Morning Updates

Lily wanted to know where everyone was, so she called for William, the speedy crow, to check on Dot, the forest critters and where all the humans were. William first found the humans, who were almost halfway to the place where Dot had run off. He reported that they should be getting there in about 45 minutes.

"Great, now go find Dot and come back as fast as you can to let me know about the puppy's ETA", she said excitedly, hoping for perfect timing.

23 * Dot and the Speeding Convoy *

Burfoot led the way with the other Scurriers and Dot, trying to make up for lost time, due to the missing log over the creek. She decided to ignore Jojo's instructions and opted to take a shortcut through an old ghost town, empty since the early 1800s. Jojo didn't like to go anywhere near the abandoned town, he felt he'd seen multiple ghosts there in the past.

As Burfoot made the turn into the

abandoned town, Jojo started to screech, but Burfoot just ignored him and kept running, leading the convoy behind her. As they approached the empty settlement, Dot was taking in all the sights. She observed the old chimney stacks, the general store sign dangling from a rusty chain, fallen fences covered in vines, the church steeple laying on the ground, and a small graveyard with weather-worn rocks were tombstones.

Dot wanted to check everything out, but Burfoot was running a fast clip, and this was no time for exploring. Dot was still following all the critters, but she wasn't watching closely where she was going as she stuck up her nose to take in the ancient musty odors. Distracted from following the squirrels, she didn't see the convoy pivot around an old wellhead that dropped into a deep hole. Dot was running, and then suddenly, she was floating, then she was, bouncing down the moss-covered stone walls of the well. Dot let out a loud howl the second she was airborne, followed by a sad little whimper as she tried to shake off all the water that soaked her. Looking around in the dark dank hole, she was grateful that her head and most of her body were not underwater.

Jeremy, who was the caboose of the squirrel train, let out the loudest squirrel bark he could muster, but no one heard him since there was so much noise from the squirrels rushing through dry, crackling leaves.

Jojo beyond upset witnessing Dot fall in the well. Even though he liked to think of himself as brave and cool as a cucumber, he didn't want to go anywhere near the ghost-town. He had major fears of the spirits that might be floating around down there. He knew he had to stop Burfoot and the others as fast as he could.

Jojo squawked louder to get the convoy's attention.

Burfoot could hear the Jojo, but she had a mantra in her head, "Get Dot to her humans. Get Dot home. Get Dot home fast". She repeated this mantra over and over. Burfoot was not going to stop or slow down for anyone. This included Jojo, so she continued to ignore his cranky squawks.

Jojo was getting incredibly frustrated, but he still felt safer up in the trees. He broke a small branch off a tree and dropped it right in front of Burfoot, squawking persistently. Burfoot wasn't fazed at all, she kept going. Finally, Jojo realized Burfoot was going to ignore him no matter what, so he called to all the crows to fly down in front of her and the other squirrels to get them to stop.

The only problem was, this convoy of squirrels just ran around the crows with their outstretched wings, like it was a fun obstacle course.

"Ignore the crows. Get Dot home. Get Dot home fast!" Burfoot ordered the squirrels, who loved the extra challenge, and giggled as they ran past the wide-eyed crows flapping their wings.

Jojo's head feathers were getting bigger and bigger the more frustrated he got with Burfoot, who was definitely not acting as a team player. Jojo saw his friend Remi, a red-tailed hawk, pointed his wing to Burfoot, and screeched, "Bring me that squirrel running in front!"

Remi dive-bombed from the tree branch and used his talons to grab Burfoot's tail. He then flew up and dropped Burfoot on the branch next to Jojo.

Burfoot was frozen with fear, she thought she was about to become this hawk's lunch. When she saw Jojo, she started pleading for her life, "Jojo, you must help me! I don't want to die, please help me, Jojo." But then she was a bit confused when the hawk simply flew away.

"Oh my goodness, that scared me so badly! I thought I was going to die. I saw my life flash in front of me. There are so many things I want to do with my life. Oh, thank goodness I am still here." Burfoot stopped talking to let her adrenaline rush settle a bit, then she noticed Jojo's head feathers were huge. "What's going on with your head, Jojo?"

Jojo's blue feathered crown was getting bigger and wilder. He pointed his wing to the gang of Scurriers, who were looking up at both of them and asked, "See anyone missing?"

Burfoot's eyes bulged twice the normal size, then she hit her forehead with her paw, squeezed her eyes shut, and let out a gasp, "Dot. Where is Dot?" Her shoulders slumped, and her chin dropping her chest, as it dawned on her that Dot was not with the crew.

"She fell into an old well, and Jeremy, a real team player, is with her", Jojo squawked at Burfoot.

Burfoot cried, "Why didn't anyone let me know?"

Jojo peered at her, wishing his eyes could shoot daggers. Burfoot was starting to notice how his plume of head feathers was continuing to get bigger by the second and how angry his eyes were. Scared, she stepped slowly backwards on the branch, trying to get away from this freakish

37

mass of angry blue feathers.

Jojo, trying his best to maintain his composure, he replied, "I tried, Jeremy tried, the crows tried. You just ignored us. This mission is a team effort. A TEAM EFFORT. But no, you are only doing what you want to do. You are running on the course you want to run. You have been ignoring my instructions from the very start. This is not about YOU! Do you understand?"

Burfoot started to shake with fear, mouth hanging wide open, staring at this hot mess of a blue bird, trying to nod her head.

Jojo continuad, "You are done! Yep, all done. I never want your help ever again. I can't take your selfish actions any longer. You are off this mission."

Jojo clumsily flew away trying to balance himself, he was not used to flying with his head feathers so puffed up, but as fast as he could, he wanted to get to a tree closer to Dot and Jeremy and away from Burfoot.

Burfoot was trying to process everything that had just happened. First, she was a hero squirrel on a mission to reunite Dot with her family, then she thought she was someone's lunch, then she just had her heart broken by being kicked off the best adventure she had ever been on. Tears bubbled up and slid down her whiskers as she watched all the other Scurriers go back to where Jeremy was looking down the well, keeping his eyes on Dot.

24 * Dot in the Well *

Dot was standing in six inches of icy water looking up the well shaft to a blue sky and was grateful to see Jeremy peeking down at her. Jeremy hollered down the hole, "Are you okay?"

Dot answered, "I don't quite know; my butt and tail are super sore. I think I lost some fur as I fell down the well. No broken bones. I am cold; the water is just below my chest, but it's freezing." She was silent for a moment then continued, "I don't know how to get out."

Jeremy, who never had any responsibility, tried as hard as he could to sound strong when he replied, "Don't you worry, we will figure it out, but it might take a minute or two. Running in place might help you to stay warm."

Jeremy looked around and realized he was all alone. Then he had a great idea and ran off to grab anything and everything he could carry. With a pile of objects next to him, Jeremy peered over the hole, yelling down, "Move to the opposite side of the hole from me." Dot did what he asked, and Jeremy started dropping down sticks, nuts, and small rocks. Then he yelled, "I will be right back." and ran off again.

By this time, Jojo had flown up above him while the rest of the squirrels were heading his way. Jeremy explained Dot's predicament to Jojo, who was sitting upon the highest branch he could find, so he didn't have to be anywhere near the spooky graveyard.

William flew up and tried to land next to Jojo, flapping his wings to get control of his landing but it took him about three times to grip the branch so he could land. He wanted to get a status report for Lily, but he was taken aback when he didn't see Dot anywhere. He coolly asked Jojo, "What's up dude?"

Jojo, whose crown of head feathers were starting to get back to normal answer, "It is not good. Dot has fallen down an old well that is about ten feet deep. The good news is that there is only about six inches of water in the well. The bad news is she is cold. And the really bad news is we haven't figured out how to get her out yet."

Jeremy shouted up, "I'm dropping small objects down into the well, so she has something to stand on, kind of like building a scaffold to get her out of the water."

"Brilliant Jeremy, just brilliant!", Jojo yelled down, then he ordered the Scurriers, who had just arrived, to help Jeremy.

Jojo said to William, "Please let Lily know we are going to need a master plan. I will try to figure how to get Dot out of this well, but we are going to need some creative problem-solving."

William nodded his head, saying, "You got it dude", then blasted back to the command center, leaving a tail feather in his wake.

25 * The Command Center *
Lunchtime

William skidded to a stop on the boulder where Lily and Rory were sitting. They were smashing walnuts with rocks for their lunchtime snack. Ruth was above in the tree working on her nest, adding fresh moss, twigs, and tree bark, getting ready for the upcoming freeze.

The trio stopped what they were doing to give their full attention to William as he squawked, "Dot fell down the old ghost town well but luckily there is only about six inches of water in it."

Rory wailed," Nooooooooo. Oh no! What are we going to do now? Should we get Squatch? Squatch can help us. We need Squatch."

Shaking her head, Lily said, "Rory, it is okay, we can figure this out ourselves. I know you really want to meet Squatch, but we've got this."

Disappointed, Rory knew Lily was right, but he was always trying to figure out a way to meet his idol. Then he snapped out of it to get back to his normal worrisome state, "Oh, what if we can't get her out and she freezes in the well and becomes a big ice cube. I can see it now, a doggy ice cube. Oh, that would be terrible."

William, Lily, and Ruth all looked at Rory, eyes slightly widened but suppressing their thoughts at his wild imagination. William continued, "The Scurriers are working to build a dry place for Dot by dropping debris down the well for her to stand on. But this delay puts us really behind schedule. There is no way Dot will be here when the humans come up the trail."

Lily nodded her head, "Okay, let's start a new plan to have Dot meet her family on the way back to town."

Lily looked at Rory for a long time thinking, then continued, "Okay Rory, go to the old ghost town, which is only about a mile from here, and along the way grab all the chipmunks, deer, and any other critters you can find that are willing to help, and get them to the ghost town. Ruth and I will be working on a solution and William will keep everyone updated as the plan develops."

26 * The Humans *
Lunchtime

Hazel and her dad stopped at the spot where Dot took off the day before to have their lunch. They hoped that the smell of their baloney sandwiches would entice Dot to return to them. They planned to walk north on the trail until three p.m. and then turn around and hurry back downtown before sunset.

Hazel was thinking about funny things Dot had done in the past. "Dad, do you remember the time that Dot was trying to play with Boris and Boris's ball?".

The Colonel laughed, "Yes, Dot had the

ball in her mouth with her front legs extended out in front of her and she was wiggling her butt and then prancing back and forth in front of Boris was sitting on her favorite table." the Colonel let out a loud belly laugh as he continued, "Then Dot got right next to the table and, lo and behold, Boris hit the framed picture of Dot off the table, and it landed right on top of Dot. It was as if Boris knew it was a picture of Dot." They both laughed at the memory. Resuming, he said, "I have never seen a cat hate a dog so much. Dot only wants to play, but grumpy old Boris just won't have anything to do with her. Well, let's hope when we find Dot that Boris will eventually learn to love her as we do." Smiling they packed up their picnic then continued up the trail.

27 * The Mean Moonshine Man * Changing the Tire

Jimbo was hoping someone would drive down the road to help him, but no luck. He started rooting around for some rocks, to put behind the tires on the rear of his truck, so he could jack up the front. He had never changed a tire on a hill before, and it scared him a bit. Not that he ever would admit to being scared.

Betty was wandering close by, trying to find grass to eat, to hopefully fill her grumbling stomach. One of the many things she didn't like about her owner was he just wasn't very concerned about food. He was fine barely eating anything, so he didn't think much about feeding her either. Every morning he would throw Betty a cup of bland dry dog food out on the ground, as if he was feeding a chicken. Unfortunately, much of the time her short chain kept her just out of reach for a fair amount of the food. At night, she could hear the opossums, mice, and raccoons enjoying his food

She dreamed of being a dog that got to live in a warm home with happy humans, bowls that were never empty of good dog food, and occasionally, being able to get a prized bone with warm steak and glistening fat. Wouldn't that be doggy heaven. These were nice thoughts, but in the meantime, she chewed on the grass, listening to her owner muttering and fussing as he struggled to change the tire.

28 * The Critters *
Old Ghost Town- Lunchtime

The Scurriers had just finished dropping down the last few leaves and William's long black tail feather into the cozy nest they were building for Dot above the chilly water in bottom of the well.

Dot had gotten a bit tired from dodging side to side while all the Scurriers were dropping stuff down for her nest, so she curled up to take a nap. Shortly after falling into a deep sleep, she was jolted out of her peaceful slumber when something bounced off her and landed right in front of her face. It was a dead, wet, slimy, fish and had very weird whiskers sticking out of its face, not to mention the protruding eyes staring blankly at her. What she didn't know was that Jojo had ordered the bald eagle to drop a freshly caught catfish from the river down the well for her lunch.

Jojo had become distracted by Burfoot jumping up and down on the fallen steeple, yelling out to him. Because he was distracted, he had forgotten to tell Jeremy to warn Dot to watch out for the fish delivery. Once he realized his mistake, his head feathers started to spring up with irritation, as he looked at Burfoot with an icy glare, blaming her for the distraction.

Frightened by the fish, Dot started barking fiercely at this intruder. Jeremy also let out a cry, as this massive fish, five times his size, went flying past him. He started bouncing side to side, as if to shake off the shock, and rapidly called down the well, "Holy moly, Dot are you okay?"

Dot continued to stare at this whiskered face and said in an undecided voice, "I think so." Then she asked, "Is this my lunch?"

Jeremy replied, "I guess so. I am so sorry no one gave us a warning. What a shocker!"

Dot reassured Jeremy, "It's okay, I am not hurt. I was only startled, but I have fish goo all over me." She started licking her paw, then pawed at her head, repeating this process over and over, attempting to get the fish slime off.

29 * The Critters *
Around the Well

Around the wellhead, a group of critters had gathered, brainstorming ideas on how to get Dot out. Buck, the deer, said, "I can hold my antlers over the well, and we could have a chain of squirrels hang from them to pull her out."

Jojo replied, "That is a nice visual, but I can't imagine that the squirrel at the top of the chain would have the strength to hold all that weight."

Morgan, Rory's brother, piped up, "I could climb down the well and she could climb on my back, and I could carry her up."

Jojo thought about it, then said, "I'm not convinced she could hang onto you."

Climbing up a tree to try to be level with Jojo, but not too close, Burfoot yelled, "Jojo, I have a great idea." Jojo ignored her, while shaking his head to try to get his head feathers to settle down, and addressed the rest of the crowd, "Okay, anyone else have some thoughts?"

A turkey gobbled, "Okay, here's a thought. We get Mr. Bobcat, here, to hold onto a couple of raccoons to carry him down the hole, and then Mr. Bobcat can gently bite down on Dot's neck and the raccoons can carry them all out."

Jojo acknowledged the turkey with a nod but then said, "That's an interesting idea, but let's keep brainstorming a bit more".

Burfoot screamed a second time, "Jojo, I have an idea!" Again, Jojo just continued to ignore her. Jojo told everyone, "Let's take a break and have a bite to eat while we continue to brainstorm." He was doing his best to ignore Burfoot's attempts to get his attention.

30 * Rory *
The Ghost Town

Worrisome Rory was so fretful that he was glad when Lily told him to go to the old ghost town. He hurried off to join the group of critters already gathered there, while inviting everyone he saw to join him, as Lily asked.

As Rory led the critters into the ghost town, he saw a massive catfish dropping from the sky landing in the well.

Rory said, "Thanks for joining us and check out what going on, but I have something very important to attend to."

But to himself he said, 'LUNCH!' Rory ran to the wellhead as fast as he could to give Dot a visit, hoping she would share. Maybe a full stomach would help him come up with a brilliant idea about how to get Dot out.

Rory yelled down the well, "I'm coming down to give you a bit of company Dot.", as he wiped away the saliva with excited anticipation of the yummy catfish.

31 * Burfoot *
Lunchtime

Burfoot's home nest was right next to a crop of super large boulders that humans would climb. She was always very fascinated that they had so many weird things tied around their bodies. It was so foreign to her because she loved to climb on everything; it was like breathing to her. So, to see these humans put on helmets, ropes, and medal hooks, just to climb rocks, made her laugh. But now, thinking about Dot, Burfoot got it. Humans and some critters just didn't have her little padded paws, her sharp claws, or her agility skills. Yet humans wanted to be able to do what she could do, like climbing trees and super large boulders, just because it was so much fun.

Burfoot wanted to let Jojo know about these rope harnesses that humans used, however Jojo was just too mad at her right now to even listen to her. She thought about how his head feathers were ginormous when he was livid with her, and she never wanted to see that again. As everyone was eating and brainstorming, Burfoot decided to see if she could find something like a rope, she could tie around herself, to try to get Jojo's attention.

She decided to search the ghost town to find what she needed, and she set off very determined. Burfoot ran into the general store where a door had once been, bounced on the dusty counters, and landed on the large, old, measuring scale sitting on the counter. She jumped up and down, loving the springs that gave the natural bounce in her step a bit more height. She jumped up and down about ten times before she remembered why she was in the store.

Burfoot shouted out loud to herself, "Mission. I am on a mission to get Dot out of the well." With extra vigor, she bounced one last time on the scale, propelling herself to the highest shelf, to get a bird's eye view of the musty old store. She observed the floor that was littered with broken jars, dirt, and leaves, big barrels, and deteriorating newspapers. But no rope.

She headed to the back storeroom, bouncing through the ajar door, but there were no windows, it was almost pitch black, with only a shimmer of light coming from the broken windows in the front of the store. Burfoot was ready to turn around when she started to fall through a hole in the wooden floor, but she managed to use her claws to grab onto the edge and drag herself up. She investigated the hole and was startled to see a group of red eyes glowing up to her.

32 * Burfoot *
The Glowing Eyes

Burfoot jumped a solid foot up and back, horrified by the dozen eyes beaming up at her from the hole in the floor. Steadying herself, she cautiously crept back to look in the hole again.

Rapidly, six young raccoons popped up out of the hole, and ran into the front room. They all turned to wait for Burfoot to come out of the dark room.

Rattled, Burfoot waited for her heartbeat to slow down to move; she peeked around the door and was taken aback with all the raccoons, staring at her. Realizing they were waiting for her, she decided to confront this gang of bandits. Figuring she could jump higher and faster than they could if they attacked.

On shaking legs, Burfoot slowly walked out, trying to act nonchalant, and said, "Howdy-do, how are you?"

Abby, the leader of the pack spoke out in a stern voice, "We want to help you. We saw everything. We saw how you were leading the team, then the dog fell into the hole, that blue jay yelled at you. You still wanted to help that dog even with that tongue-lashing. Yep, we want to help." Changing her voice to be incredibly sarcastic, "But our dad, Morgan, wants us to stay out of the way. To be safe and stay in our hidey-hole. Because there are so many critters around. Well, we don't want to stay down no stinking hole with all this action going on. Whatever you need, we are here to help."

Burfoot looked at them, clapped her paws together rejoicing, and said "Oh yeah baby, I would love your help." She continued, "Here's what we're going to do, and this is what we're on the lookout for."

33 * Rory & Dot *
Down the Well

Rory climbed down the well, tail first, negotiating each rock with his paws as he eased his way down.

"Hey Dot. I'm Rory. I want to keep you company down here and see if we could figure out how to get you back up on dry land." He was trying to control his excitement as the aroma of the fish became stronger the closer, he got.

Dot wiggled her tiny tail with excitement to have some company and jumped up on Rory, licking his face with sloppy, wet kisses.

"Slow down and please stop. I am a bit scared of germs.", Rory pleaded.

Dot stopped licking, but she couldn't slow down, so she stood there wiggling her whole body.

Spotting the fish, he continued, "Do you mind if I have a nibble?"

Dot nodded her head. Rory started eating and talking about all that was going on, including the man in the red truck, the orange cat, the crows, Lily, and everyone above them.

After about 30 minutes, Rory realized he had snarfed down most of the fish. He stopped talking to observe Dot, to see if she had noticed how much of the fish he had gobbled up, which she had not. Then he slowly started to work on the remaining meat, trying to leave Dot a nice, but small, portion.

34 * Burfoot *
The Adolescent Raccoons

Abby and the rest of the adolescent
raccoons heard Burfoot out. Abby looked at her
siblings and said, "Okay, I think we should all split
up to look for a rope or cord of some kind but,
whatever you do, don't let Papa Morgan see you!
This store will be our meeting place. Let's
plan on meeting back here after we've
canvassed the whole town." Abby looked at her
brother Morgan Jr. and said, "You stay put so
everyone can report to you." Morgan Jr. nodded
his head and was positively relieved because he
never wanted to upset his papa. Everyone except
Morgan Jr. left the old store, darting in different
directions, on a treasure hunt for a rope.

35 * Jojo *
After Lunch-The Ghost town

Jojo was getting a bit frustrated because
he was always a quick problem solver. He just
couldn't quite figure out a solution to this
dilemma. The longer he went without a tactical
plan, the smaller his crown of blue feathers
shrunk, and his interior beat weakened. He

decided to fly around believing the ghost town was messing with his mind. As he lifted off, he noticed dark shadows skirting around the edges of the sagging buildings which freaked him out that much more. He felt like he couldn't get out of there fast enough, so he decided to visit Lily; maybe she could help him.

36 * Burfoot and the Raccoons * Dark Shadows

The dark shadows skirting about the old town were in fact Abby, her siblings, and Burfoot, trying to stay hidden from Papa Morgan and the rest of the critters.

As they hugged the shadows of different structures, one sibling went to an old shed, one went into a dilapidated house, and one darted around the crumbling tombstones in the small, lonely graveyard. Burfoot and Abby both went into the musty church with the fallen steeple outside. They started sneezing, from dust, but they continued to run down the center aisle to the alter, both looked around, and saw stairs in the back leading up to the choir loft. They sprinted up the stairs, and saw another set of stairs, which they both raced up. Abruptly, stopping on the top stair, they froze in shock at what was in front of them.

37 * Jojo & Lily *
Command Center

Jojo flew down into Lily's den, where Lily was arranging the different nuts and mushrooms, she had been collecting for the past few months. Jojo, feeling humiliated, landed on a log that Lily had brought into her den. Lily looked up in delight to see her good friend, saying, "To what do I owe the great pleasure for your visit, my friend?"

Jojo replied, "I am puzzled. I just don't know how to get Dot out of that deep hole. I'm so humiliated, that my fear of ghosts, is the reason I can't think straight. I'm so ashamed!" Saying this, he fell on his back, covered his head with his wings, and let out an anguished cry.

Lily had known Jojo for years and never, ever, had she seen him so despondent. Just seeing him this distressed, brought tears to her eyes, her brow furrowed with worry. She took a deep breath and sat on the floor so she could be eye to eye with him. In a calm voice she said, "Jojo, we have had many missions together helping both critters and people, and you have always been a wonderful leader. I know you will be successful on this mission, too. What we need is a rope, or vines, to tie around Dot and have all the critters pull her out. It is that simple. I was going to ask William to tell you this the next time he stopped by for my updates. I apologize for not summoning him sooner. Jojo, go back and have all the critters you can get, to go into the woods to collect vines to create a rope."

Jojo removed one of his wings to look at Lily. His crown of feathers started to spring up. His head started to bob again, very slightly. He rolled over and got up, lifting his wings and his internal beat switched on. He started bobbing and strutting. He looked at Lily, flew up to her shoulders, wrapped his wings around her neck, for a grateful hug.

As she watched him fly off, fresh tears moistened her eyes but this time it was for love. She looked up to Ruth and gave her a wink. She knew she was blessed to have so many wonderful friends.

38 * Burfoot and Abby * Church

At the top of the stairs, Burfoot and Abby stopped abruptly, staring at just what they were looking for. A long, golden, husky rope hanging down from a big brass bell. It was dazzling. They both did a happy dance around the rope. Abby's tail accidentally hit the rope causing the bell to ring. They both grabbed the rope at the same time to stop the noise, staring at each other with wide eyes, beaming grins, and giggling joyously.

Burfoot said, "Okay, we found it! But how the heck do we get it down? I'm going to go up there to see how it is attached. Hold the rope tight for me."

Abby grabbed the rope and Burfoot

scurried up it, reaching the top, she yelled down, "It is a tight knot, let me see if I can loosen it." She pulled and pulled, but the rope didn't budge.

Burfoot sighed with frustration and yelled again, "I am coming down, hold tight."

Once she landed back on the floor, Burfoot said, "I think I'll need to chew the rope until it falls. Hold the rope while I go up again and then go tell Morgan Jr. to get all your siblings to come here while I start to get my teeth through this old rope."

Abby said, "Sounds like a plan. See you shortly."

39 * The Mean Moonshine Man *
On The Road Again

After finally mounting the spare tire, Jimbo threw the flat tire, rusty jack, and tire-iron in the back of the truck. He hollered, "Come on Betty, git in the truck.", as he patted his seat by the steering wheel, holding the door open for her. She happily jumped into the cab of the truck, grateful at not having to be in the back anymore, the cold and the stinky moonshine.

"We gotta git some dry wood back at the house, and finish our deliveries.", Jimbo continued. But Betty was only half-heartedly listening as she closed her eyes, happy to have some of the warmth that was slowly trickling out from the old truck heater. As they drove away, a trail of moonshine marked their path.

40 * Jojo and The Critters *
Ghost Town

Jojo called for all the critters to gather around, then told them to roam around and find as many vines as they could; the crows were to fly around to monitor everyone's progress. Everyone was so happy to finally be doing something that there was a rumble of excited chatter as they left.

Rory heard the buzz of excitement followed by silence. He climbed out of the well to find out what was going on. Once there, he saw no one. It really did feel like a ghost town. He was exhausted from climbing to the top with his bulging belly, stuffed to the gills with catfish. He decided to lay down on his back and wait for someone to come back and inform him what was going on. Dot on the other hand, decided to sleep while she waited, content to have the last bit of catfish filling her little puppy tummy.

41 * Burfoot Nibbling *

Burfoot was nibbling away on the rope, cutting through each thin fiber, one by one. After every ten fibers, she would pause to look at her work. It felt like her progress was so slow that she would never get through the entire rope. She perked up when Abby and her siblings came into the bell tower.

Abby yelled up to Burfoot, "Hey, I overheard Jojo telling all the critters to go look for vines, so basically, they have the same idea as us. I really want to get that rope down fast so we can get Dot out before they get back.", she announced.

Burfoot's head lifted like a fierce warrior, cheering, "I love that goal! Let's do it."

"I love it!" Abby replied, "Okay, let's take turns."

Burfoot ran down and Abby ran up, each holding the rope tight for the other. The fibers of the rope were flying everywhere as all the siblings and Burfoot were taking turns gnawing through the tough rope. Burfoot was back up when she realized that she only had a few tendrils of rope remaining. Suddenly, it dawned on her that she had been climbing up and down her only path, the rope, and soon it would be on the ground in a big heap.

SNAP!!!

The siblings darted for their lives. The rope fell, hitting the floor with a loud thud. Burfoot was still high above, clinging onto the round bell clapper that the rope had been tied to. She swung side to side in the bell, which was making a dull thudding sound as Burfoot kept shifting her body side to side, to stop the clapper from hitting the bell.

Once the bell clapper came to a rest, Burfoot looked at the twenty-foot drop, then at Abby, and then to the walls, that were all about three feet away. Calculating in her mind, Burfoot

knew she needed a good leap to get to one of the walls but hanging onto the bell clapper was not going to give her a good push off point. She also knew that the brass bell was not ideal material for her to get a good grip on. Burfoot looked down to see five pairs of banded eyes
staring up at her, as she continued to swing back and forth. She yelled down, "I got this." Holding onto the little bit of rope that was still connected to the clapper, she started a controlled swing. When she felt the swing was just right, she released her grip on the rope and used her momentum to her fly to the wall. She nailed the landing like an Olympic gymnast, with a perfect "TEN". However, the act of jumping with all her might pushed the clapper away from her into the opposite side of the bell. **BONG, BONG, BONG**, the sound was ear-splitting and brain paralyzing.

Stunned, Burfoot fell off the wall, her brain jiggling like jelly. She landed on all the siblings, who were piled up together tightly, their paws covering their ears to block out the brain-shattering noise.

As the bell quieted down, the siblings and Burfoot were slowly shaking their heads, poking their toes into their ears to try to stop the ringing in their heads. Suddenly, they all saw a dark figure in the door, and their eyes widened as they became mute with fear.

Rory looked down at his nieces, nephews, and Burfoot in a big pile, still shaking their heads. The young raccoons were staring in fright at their Uncle Rory, because Rory and their dad Morgan were very close. They knew their uncle would tell on them.

In union, the raccoons cried out, **"Oh Nooooo!!!"**

Rory could only chuckle to himself, seeing his sweet family. Rory knew that his brother was strict with his kids because he wanted to protect them. He, also, remembered
all the trouble he and his brother used to get into when *they* were young. Rory's worrisome self, faded away; he had been frightened by a the noise of the bell, but now he was relieved to see that his nieces, nephews, and Burfoot were all together.

Rory boomed out, "What in the world are you are doing up here making all this racket?"

Shaking like a leaf, Abby stood up, "Hey, Uncle Rory. We wanted to help Burfoot and Dot. We found this awesome rope that we want to tie around Dot to pull her out."

They all stared at Rory to see what his reaction would be. Rory let out a jovial laugh, and their fears evaporated. With a huge wave of relief, they all clamored to show him the rope.

Rory was so happy that his nieces, nephews, and Burfoot had found the rope. He ordered, "Alright, let's get this long rope over to help Dot." With a spring in their steps, they each grabbed a section of rope and headed down the stairs.

42 * The Well *
Tug-a-Dot

Dot could hear happy chatter up above, when Rory yelled down, "We are coming to get you Dot. First, we are going to lower a rope to you, and then we will be down there in a second."

All the young raccoons, Burfoot, and Rory started to inch the rope down, paw over paw. Rory lifted his paw in an upward fist, so all the critters knew that the end had reached Dot. A spontaneous cheer broke out. Rory looked at his family and said, "Okay, I want everyone to hang on tight", he directed his family. "Burfoot and I are going down."

Burfoot was so excited, she sprinted down the stone wall of the well, followed by Rory, who was a bit slower, but just as excited. Burfoot, getting close to Dot, jumped on Dot's back and wrapped all her tiny little legs around Dot's thick neck, hugging her tightly. "I am so sorry Dot! I feel so bad for what happened to you. It is all my fault."

Dot was shaking with so much enthusiasm that Burfoot could not hold on any longer and she fell off the wiggling dog. Dot spun around and started licking the regretful squirrel. Burfoot tried to continue to apologize, but it was hard to talk with Dot's huge wet tongue, which was bigger than Burfoot's head, licking her non-stop. Not to mention all the wet slobber flying everywhere.

Rory finally got to the bottom of the well, and said, "Okay, you two, let's get to work." Dot stopped licking Burfoot and gave her undivided attention to Rory.

Burfoot was soaking wet from Dot's slobber which reeked with a strong fishy odor. She was trying to wipe her face clean with her front legs and paws while trying not to gag from the smell. Dog breath is one thing, but fishy dog breath is something else!

Rory barked, "Burfoot, are you paying attention?" Burfoot nodded her head, even though she was still distracted from feeling so slimy. "Okay, Dot, this is what we are going to do", he went on to explain how they were going to tie the rope around her and lift her out of the well. Both Burfoot and Rory worked together to tie the rope around Dot. It took them about three times to feel comfortable that the knots would hold while lifting Dot.

Rory ordered, "Burfoot, go to the top and have everyone to start to pull."

Burfoot responded, "No, you go to the top and start to pull. You are a lot stronger than me."

Rory countered back, "Yes I am much stronger, and I am bigger, so if something happens to Dot, I can protect her better if she falls."

Burfoot grumbled, "Fine.", and ran up the rock wall. Once she was at the top, she found a pile of raccoons sleeping on top of the rope. Burfoot surveyed the surroundings to see what was going on, and who was around. She noticed that Morgan Jr. was peering out the broken window of the general store and she gave him a thumbs up. Burfoot then noticed Buck, a large white-tailed deer, eating grass at the edge of town.

Feeling it was safe, she woke up all the siblings, and said, "Alright, team, let's get to work. Each of you grab ahold of the rope, and on the count of three we will start to pull." They all got into formation, Burfoot counted, "Okay, one, two, three, pull.", they continued to pull and count.

Burfoot was on the rope closest to the hole and Abby was at the tail end of the rope. Burfoot yelled down to Rory, "How far up the wall is she?"

Rory yelled up, "Only about five inches, can't you all go faster? This is going to take all night, and we are still trying to get Dot to her family today before the sun sets."

Hearing this Abby turned around and hollered to her brother Morgan Jr., "Come over and help us, Morgan!"

Her brother opened his eyes wide and shook his head.

Abby yelled again, "Come on!"

More head shaking from Morgan Jr.

Abby shouted, "Dad is not here, you can help us."

Abby waited for him to come out, but when she looked at the store, she could see the tips of his ears fading to the back of the store. As they continued to pull, Abby was very frustrated with Morgan Jr, and this gave her a bit of extra pulling strength. Suddenly, she noticed a large dark shadow looming over her. Abby slowly looked up to see what was creating the shadow looming above. To her surprise, she saw Buck, the deer that had been eating grass close by.

He looked at her saying, "It looks like you could use a little help here."

Abby grinned from ear to ear, saying, "Oh yeah!" Then she yelled, "Burfoot, we have some help."

Burfoot turned around and rejoiced, "Why did I not include Buck when I first saw him?" Then she yelled down the well, "Hold on a minute, we have something that might help us go faster."

Dot was hanging about eight inches above Rory, who was getting nervous and, of course, hungry.

Dot replied, "No problem, I'm just hanging

out."

Rory yelled, "Hurry up, I am getting hungry!"

Burfoot instructed Abby's siblings to bunch together, and to hold on tight to the part of the rope closest to the opening of the well. She looked at Buck, and asked, "Would you mind if we tied this rope to your antlers?"

Good old Buck responded, "Well it would be my pleasure, Ms. Burfoot, and I will be happy to lower my head for ya". He turned around, facing away from the well.

Burfoot signaled for Abby, and together they tied the rope securely around Buck's antlers. Burfoot said to Buck, "Sir, we are done. Would you mind if I stayed close to the knot in the rope, to keep an eye on it?" Buck replied, "Sure thing, Ms. Burfoot".

At that moment Rory started yelling up the well, "Burfoot what the heck is going on up there?".

Burfoot stationed herself on Buck's antler, as if she were on a horse. Holding onto the knotted rope, she yelled, "Giddy up, Buck!" Buck lifted his two front legs, doing a little dance in the air, then landed on all fours and galloped towards the general store. Within seconds Dot was pulled out of the well.

Dot yelled "Yee ha!"

"Wow, she shot out of here like a shooting star!", Rory celebrated.

43 * Jojo and The Critters *
Vines

Jojo and the crows flew above all the critters to see how they were doing, collecting an assortment of vines. Jojo was satisfied that the bundles of vines everyone had were sufficient. He and the crows passed the word for everyone to head back to the ghost town with their new loot.

The squirrels, chipmunks, Morgan, a few deer, the turkey, Mr. Bobcat, and others, all worked together to get the vines back to Dot.

44 * The Well *
Ghost Town

Standing on solid ground never felt so good to Dot, she started yapping with joy and excitement. She jumped up and down, then started doing a happy run, back and forth, with such glee that she did not even realize she was tripping up all the young raccoons, who were laughing and trying to jump over the rope she was dragging around.

"How do you do, Ms. Dot?" Buck asked the little black and white puppy who was darting around like a Tasmanian devil.

"Great!", Dot replied, looking directly up at Buck. "Thank you", she continued, as she repeated it to each of the raccoon siblings, Burfoot, and finally to Rory, as he climbed out of the well. "I am so grateful, and so lucky, to have so many great friends taking care of me." Everyone was basking in the good feelings.

Suddenly a chilly wind swept across the town as Jojo landed on a branch just above them, immediately bringing everyone to a standstill.

"Burfoot, I told you to go away and to leave us alone." Jojo thundered.

45 * The Ghost Town *
The Standoff

Critters were coming into the ghost town from different directions, dragging along the vines, but there was a cold chill in the air when they reached the edge of town.

The chill was from Jojo, but ironically, he was sizzling hot with anger. His crown of feathers started to explode into a momentous plume, pushing out all the tiny little feathers, which created a smoky haze around him.

To boot, there was a piercing cry on the edge of the ghost town. "AAAh! What's going on here?", roared Papa Morgan, who had just swagger in from the darkened woods, horrified to see his kids outside.

Burfoot and all the siblings, including

Morgan Jr., who was still hiding in the old store, went from jubilee to panic, seeing Jojo and Papa Morgan.

A lone crow let out a long cry flying overhead.

The tension was thick, like an old western stand-off. Everyone was looking at each other, heads going back and forth. You could hear a pin drop.

Jeremy, the caboose of the squirrel train, who was next to Morgan, was gripping his vines so tightly that the vines snapped, making a loud sound. Morgan darted his angry eyes at him. Backing up slowly at first, Jeremy dropped the vines, turned around, and ran up the nearest tree as fast as he could.

"Stop! Stop this right now!", yelled Rory, as he stood up on his two hind legs while pointing his little fingers at both Jojo and Papa Morgan.

"We are a team, a great critter posse, and we support each other. We are going to be a team that works together and forgives each other. So, we all need to listen to each other. Jojo, Burfoot feels really bad about what happened to Dot. But it was her idea to find a rope to get Dot out. Big brother Morgan, I love you, but your kids are awesome. They definitely don't need to be hiding in a hole, just because that makes you feel safe. Burfoot and the kids are superheroes right now, and you need to give them a sincere 'thank you'. Buck also deserves our heartfelt gratitude, for generously sharing his strength."

"Thank you, thank you very much." Buck replied, "I was quite honored to help y'all."

Jojo, reluctantly, became reflective, realizing that he was acting like a jerk about Burfoot, and knew that Rory was right.

"Thanks, Burfoot, and I am sorry I refused to listen to you. Also, thanks to Morgan's kids and to you, Mr. Buck", Jojo said in a forgiving tone as his crown of feathers began to deflate.

Dot was just staring at everyone with wide happy eyes while dancing with happiness.

Morgan started to walk up to stare seriously at his kids, but he became panic-stricken when he didn't see all his kids, one was missing.

"Where's Jr?", Morgan bellowed.

The siblings, Burfoot, and Buck, all faced the old general store, and if you looked closely, you could see the very tips of Morgan Jr.'s ears quivering at the bottom of a window.

Morgan yelled, "Son, get out here." Slowly, Morgan Jr. came out, and Morgan yelled again, "Hurry up!" Finally, Jr. reached all his siblings. "Well, I am proud of you kids", Morgan said with a sigh of relief. "Y'all aren't toddlers anymore, I need to remember that. Your mama would be proud." All the siblings ran to Papa Morgan, knocking him down, to give him a whole bunch of affection. Dot, too, wanted to be a part of this happy celebration. She jumped right on top of the pile of raccoons, giving everyone fishy kisses.

"Okay, enough of all this love fest, we need to get this show on the road. Burfoot and everyone, get these ropes off Buck and Dot", ordered Rory. He then looked up to Jojo, who nodded his head.

Jojo was feeling a great sense relief to be leaving the ghost town. He couldn't wait. Looking at the sun, he figured they had about 3 hours until sunset, and hoped they would find the family before dark.

"Jojo, we need to talk", Rory said, as he signaled to his friend, who still would not lower himself off the highest branch. "Meet me in the woods over there", he pointed. Rory wanted to have a conversation with Jojo, without having to yell at the treetops.

The funny thing about Rory, was when he needed to be strong and bossy he would rise to the occasion. When he wasn't in charge, that's when he had too much time to think, getting himself, all worked up with worry and hunger.

Flying into the woods, Jojo landed on a baby dogwood tree and waited for Rory to arrive.

"Jojo, you need to start trusting Burfoot again." Rory said. "She is young and has made some mistakes. While this may surprise you, she is just as smart as you are. We always need talent like that."

Jojo cocked his head, a bit concerned that his crown of feathers was going to act up again.

Rory continued, "All she needs is some mentoring. Morgan's kids are awesome, too. The more fearless team players we have, the stronger we are. You were young once too. Remember?"

Jojo started nodding his head, as his internal music started playing again with a low beat.

"Rory, you are right", said Jojo, as he recalled all the silly mistakes he had made when he was a young. "Let's go back and get this show on the road."

Jojo nodded his head as his head feather rose to their correct size.

Once they got back to the ghost town, Rory announced, "Burfoot, you are on the lead, again. But slow down to make sure you have everyone. At all times! Okay?"

Burfoot looked up at Jojo with a smile and gave him a thumbs up. Jojo just looked at her, nodding his head while thinking about a beat, to make sure his crown feathers stayed down.

Seeing William fly up, Jojo gave him the update and William shot off to inform Lily of Dot's rescue from the well.

46 * The Messenger Crows *

After listening to William, Lily asked the messenger crows to pass around the information to Rusty and Rose and the group of Scurriers, who were all following Hazel and the Colonel. The group of crows following the mean moonshine man also got the good news. They were watching Jimbo at his home as he refilled his truck with dry firewood. Another group of messenger crows headed over to Dot's house to update Barney, the barred owl, and the crows watching over Dot's home. Barney looked over to Boris, who stayed by the window on the table so he could keep an eye out for any new information. When they made eye contact, Boris sensed that Dot was okay. With the knowledge that Dot was safe, the owl and the cat went back to sleep.

Lily loved that her team communicated like a well-oiled machine. However, as the day was waning, she was a bit worried that they were running out of time to reunite Dot with her family.

She and Ruth decided to go north on

her secret trail which ran parallel to the Appalachian Trail. She needed to stretch her legs and Ruth could flex her wings. They also hoped to catch up with Rusty, Rose, and the Scurriers.

47 * The Colonel and Hazel *
New Boots

Hazel had decided to wear her new hiking boots thinking the temperature was dropping and the boots would be warmer than her sneakers. Boy was that a huge mistake. She was doing her best to not complain, but her dad noticed that she was starting to limp.

"What's up, Sweet Pea? You're slowing down and limping", said the Colonel.

"I have a blister on my heel. It's not too bad. Dot is much more important." Hazel told her dad.

"Let's take a look", the Colonel said.

Hesitantly, Hazel looked at her dad with a bit of sadness because she knew he would want to turn around and go home. She only wanted to find Dot. She sat down, untied her stiff, new, boots and slowly removed the sock from her left foot, since that heel didn't feel so bad.

Her dad chuckled and said, "I saw you limping with your right foot. Let me see that one."

Even more slowly, Hazel peeled off the sock from her right foot and lifted her leg up so her dad could see.

He let out a heavy sign and said, "I am so

sorry, that looks very painful."

Hazel nodded her head then said, "Dad, I don't want to go back. Please, let's continue to look for Dot. Please."

The Colonel was frustrated with himself. He had been so worried about Dot that he had forgotten to follow several of his normal hiking rules and had not shared these with his daughter. Even simple rules, like 'never wear new boots on a long hike' and 'always carry a first aid kit'.

"Ugh, sweetie, I am so sorry that I didn't even notice you were wearing new boots. I forgot to bring a first aid kit. Your right heel has a blister the size of a silver dollar, and it's bloody. It hurts me to see you in pain. We really do need to turn around. I know you are worried, but we can come back tomorrow." She nodded, knowing he was right.

"Hazel, put your socks and boots back on since it is cold, but leave the boots as loose as you can. Now, you carry my backpack and I'll carry you as much as I can, but you will have to walk some too." Hazel did as her dad asked, climbed on his back and they headed south, back to the car.

48 * Lily and Ruth * Hidden Trail

Lily and Ruth were following the hidden trail, when they both saw Rusty, Rose, and all the Scurriers coming towards them. "What's going on? Why are you heading south?" Lily asked Rusty.

Rusty told them that Hazel had two bad blisters on her heels due to her new boots, and now they were heading back to their car.

"Oh, this is not good" Lily said as her heart sank a little bit. "This is going to be tight."

Ruth let out a loud "Caw!", in agreement.

"Ruth, go tell Jojo they need to step up the pace." Ruth nodded and took off to find the convoy.

49 * The Convoy of Critters * Heading back to the Trail

The convoy of critters were heading east, in the direction of Lily's den, when Ruth flew up parallel with Jojo as he was flying through the trees. "Jojo", she cawed, "Tell everyone to pull over by that black cherry tree so I can give everyone the update."

Jojo let out a loud call, and everyone looked up at him; he looked so relieved to see that Burfoot was listening to him.

"Hold up everyone, I need to chat with Ruth for a bit. Get some water in the stream, and I'll be right back with you." Feeling good about his improving crew, Jojo flew over to Ruth.

"Everything okay?", Jojo asked

"The family is heading back sooner than we thought, so the convoy needs to go south, to the town's approach trail."

"Sure thing, not a problem." Jojo got very excited hearing this news. He loved being in town as there was always live music. He could hear fiddles, banjos, guitars, and his favorite sound, a rhythmic drumbeat.

"How much time do you think we have?", Jojo asked.

"Not long, we really need to hustle", Ruth replied.

Jojo started bopping his head and squawked out new orders to the convoy as he watched Ruth fly off.

50 * The Convoy of Critters *
And the Humans

An hour or so after meeting with Ruth, the convoy of critters ran as fast as possible without leaving anyone behind. Some of the squirrels found it was faster for them to run in the trees, jumping from branch to branch. Burfoot stayed by Dot, with Jeremy continuing as a caboose, bringing up the rear.

Rory was so nervous about the family leaving early that he headed to Lily's den so he could eat something to calm his nerves, food always did the trick; he didn't want to slow the other critters down.

Jojo called out again, and everyone slowed to listen. "The trail is just ahead. We're going to get as close as we can without being seen. Dot, as soon as we see your family, that will be your que to run ahead. But wait for my orders, okay?" Everyone cheered, being so excited that the mission was almost finished.

Crows were flying back and forth to keep their eyes on the family, the foxes, and Dot's running convoy. Ruth decided to park herself by the railroad tracks and the approach trail. She could see the Colonel and Hazel starting to get close, and the crows flying above the trees signaling that the convoy was not far behind.

Rusty was getting upset; he didn't think they had time to reunite the family because he had an ear out listening to the crows.

Rose begged her dad, "Let me just go out there and run on the trail to slow the humans down. I'll do my best tricks."

Rusty nodded, because he knew everyone got excited to see a fox kit playing in the wild. Rose ran out to the trail and started bouncing on the ground with her two front paws as if she were trying to find a mouse in the ground, then she rolled on her back, doing her best somersaults.

"Dad, isn't this little fox the cutest!" Hazel said, laughing at Rose's antics. They both laughed as the Colonel took out his phone to record the fox kit. They paused for five minutes enjoying Rose's hilarious actions.

"Okay, hop on, we need to go.", the Colonel said to Hazel, wanting to get home so he could take care of her heels.

"Bye foxy, thanks for bringing us joy.", Hazel said, as she hopped on her dad's back.

51 * The Critters *
Getting Close

Dot was so excited about getting back to her family. She let out a little bark when she could smell a small scent of her humans on the trail. She thought she could see them through the trees. With an extra spring in her step, she started to pass Burfoot, but Burfoot grabbed Dot's stubby tail and said, "Slow down, I'm still leading, and will not let you get into trouble again!"

However, when Dot spotted the bright orange backpack on Hazel, there was no way that Burfoot could hold her back. Dot was running like she had never run before. You couldn't even see her feet hit the ground she was running so fast.

As Dot was leaving Burfoot in her dust, Burfoot cried out, "**Jojoooooooooo!!!!**". Jojo was on it, and this time he wasn't mad at Burfoot. All the crows were circling in the sky. Round and round they went, making so much racket with their cawing that townspeople were pointing and staring at the birds.

The Colonel and Hazel could hear the whistle of the tourist train approaching, and they could smell the smoke of the steam engine. "Hold on, I am going to run so we don't have to wait on this train." the Colonel said as he broke into a jog to get over the tracks.

The next time, Dot saw her family, they

were climbing into the car. She could almost smell the leather seats. Dot tried to push herself harder. Seeing her family made her heart soar with love, sadness, regret, and joy.

Meanwhile, the train was getting closer and very loud. Ruth and Jojo both saw that if Dot didn't stop, the train would hit her.

Ruth did her alarm "CAW-CAW!", which all the crows mimicked as loudly as they could, over the trains loud steam whistle.

Rusty, Rose, and the Scurriers had just watched the family get in their car. They could barely hear Ruth and the other crows over the huffing and chuffing noises of the old locomotive.

Rusty and Rose saw Dot running full bore, oblivious to the approaching train. Rusty saw that if he didn't stop Dot, she would be hit by the train.

"Come on Rose.", he yelled. They ran to Dot as fast as they could to save her life.

When Dot finally saw the train, she barked, "I can make it!" and kept running even while all the critters where screaming, "STOP!".

Rusty ran faster than he ever had. He could see the shiny metal wheels getting larger as they approached.

The train conductor saw this little puppy heading right towards him and began blaring the whistle to warn her.

BAM! Dot was hit!

Dot had the breath knocked out of her and was seeing stars. She didn't know what had hit her. Shaking her head to try to clear her starry brain. She looked up to see Rusty and Rose's golden eyes staring down at her. It was the fox duo who had knocked Dot away from the train, a split second before Dot and the train would have collided. Rose, who was finally not bored, gave

Dot a huge lick on her face. Dot's eyes went from shock, to confusion, to disbelief to sadness. Seeing the train roll by, she knew she had lost her chance to reunite with her family.

Rusty saw her sadness and lowered his head.

Jojo crash-landed on a branch, barely hanging on. For a second, he felt like he didn't have a heartbeat.

Ruth's anxiety was so high that an assortment of her feathers scattered in the breeze from the train.

Burfoot and Jeremy ran up and stared at Dot, just to make sure she was okay.

Above Dot, the branches were shaking from the squirrels who were quivering with fright.

The crows lost their voices from the shock of the near disaster.

It was a very close call.

52 * The Mean Moonshine Man * Chores Done

Jimbo was feeling a bit better, now that he had made all his firewood and moonshine deliveries for the day. Although he was still smarting over the inventory he had lost. He was driving into the drug store parking lot when he saw the father and daughter getting into their fancy car, so he rolled up next to them, just as they were driving away. He was looking for the dog, but he didn't see it anywhere. An evil smile spread across his weathered face.

"Betty girl.", he yelled to the back of the truck, and she perked up her ears as she huddled under the moist tarp. "Our mission is still on." Jimbo hooted with an evil laugh as he parked his truck.

The crows started to do their distress call again, to alert the other critters about the man in the truck. The critters didn't hear the crows, since their ears were still ringing from the sound of the train whistle.

Jimbo put Betty on a leash and went to the trailhead as the last few cars of the train rolled by. People were waving at him. Jimbo just ignored the friendly tourists and pulled his dirty old hat down low over his face. On the other hand, or paw, sweet Betty wagged her tail and had a silly 'dog' smile on her face. After the caboose went by, Jimbo jumped over the tracks, and pulled out Dot's toys for Betty to smell. Then he said, "Find it girl." Immediately she howled, "Ah-Roooooo". At first, the mean moonshine man thought his dog was letting out a false alert. But then, he saw Dot in the woods right off the approach trail. Plus, he saw a slew of forest animals swarming around Dot. What he didn't know was that the critters were all pleading with Dot to stay away from him.

Burfoot was running up a tree while making loud warning sounds.

Jojo was screeching with all his might, and soon all the critters were screaming, **"Danger! Danger! Stranger Danger!"**

Then Jimbo pulled out Dot's favorite toy, the rope monkey.

Dot lifted her nose and gave a huge sniff.

That is when she lost it. That monkey was her toy! It had all her home scents on it: the Colonel, the babies, Hazel, home cooked meals, and even the cat, Boris. Dot bolted straight toward to this man, dreaming of going home. She couldn't wait to be surrounded by all her favorite smells.

The birds continued to screech, the squirrels started going nuts making different barking sounds, the foxes released murderous screams, the chipmunks squeaked as loud as they could. Ruth wailed a long painful plea.

Dot didn't hear any of it. Jimbo heard all the racket and thought it was weird, but he was solely focused on Dot.

Betty was engrossed with the critter sounds as she inhaled all the scents. She was smiling because she loved being around so many cool critters. Yet she was confused, since the critters seemed to be so upset.

Dot reached the moonshine man, who was holding her toys out for her. She grabbed the monkey's leg with her teeth in a battle of tug-a-war with him. Dot was feeling so much glee, playing with her favorite toy.

Jojo was so mad that his head feathers were in full explosion mode. He knew, from the tip of his beak to the end of his tail feathers, this man couldn't be trusted. So, he dive-bombed the moonshine man, knocking off his hat.

Irate, Ruth, blasted down after Jojo and as soon as the man lost his hat, Ruth ejected a liquid bomb of bird poop right on top of the man's head, dripping into his few remaining scraggly gray hairs.

Not wanting to miss out, Burfoot ran over, slipped inside the moonshine man's pant leg, and started biting his knee.

Jimbo was still playing tug-a-war with Dot, while shaking his leg to try to get rid of Burfoot, attempting to wipe off his head, and to pick up his hat, all at the same time. He finally managed to shake Burfoot out of his pant leg. He yelled to Betty, "Come on girl. We need to git out of here". Dropping the dog toys, grabbing Dot in his arms, he ran to the truck.

Dot wimped for her toys and finally, becoming aware of the warning calls. It was too late, the smelly man grabbed her with a vise-like grip as he darted through the parking lot. Dot let out a fearsome howl, "**Oh, Nooooooooo!**"

Burfoot and all the Scurriers tried their best to trip the old man.

Ruth flew down grabbing the strap of his overalls, but he just knocked her away. She was grateful to at least bite his finger.

As Jimbo was running, all the crows started circling above him, making the loudest noises they could. The moonshine man ran over the railroad tracks, to his truck. He opened the door, threw Dot in, and yelled for Betty to get into the cab. There wasn't time to get her in the bed of the truck.

The squawking crows were circling the truck and people staring and pointing at the weird behavior of these birds. The rest of the critters sadly watched the truck drive away.

With heavy wings and a broken heart, Ruth flew up the trail to tell Lily the bad news. Sneezing from the stinky exhaust spewing from the old truck as it sped away, she did her best to fly up from the stench.

53 * Lily's Den *
The Command Center
Dinner Time

All the critters were either crammed inside Lily's den or hanging out on the boulders and branches near the entrance. As the sun set, the mood was somber. Lily made sure everyone had something to eat.

With nothing to do, Rory started his typical nervous verbal rant, "What are we going to do now? I just knew something was going to go wrong. But, no, everyone wants to assume everything is fine. Well, is it fine? Did it work out today? No. No. No! Oh, how did this get so messed up? I hate when things don't go as planned!" He paused to catch his breath while cramming as many acorns and earthworms as possible into his mouth. Everybody was watching Rory intently. He looked back at everyone and screamed, **"What are we going to do???"** Chunks of earthworms and acorns spewed from his mouth as he asked his agitated questions.

Lily and Ruth looked at Rory, both shaking their heads. Lily took command and said, "Okay, everyone, let's calm down and come up with a plan together."

Everyone that was in Lily's underground bunker climbed out and surrounded Lily.

"If you worked today, you did an excellent job. Unfortunately, not all the luck was on our side. The good news is, we know where the moonshine man lives, which is about eight miles from here. The bad news is, he lives on the other side of the river. Day crew, I am going to ask all of you to get a good night's rest; the night crew will try to rescue Dot from the moonshine man."

"What about me? I can work at night. I want to be there too.", Rory begged.

Looking at Rory, Lily noticed that he was a disgusting mess, with worm juice all over his face, chest, and paws. Plus, it looked like he had gained ten pounds in just one day. Not to mention, his eyes were wide, bloodshot, and getting crazier looking by the second.

Lily said, "No Rory, I love how invested you are for Dot, but I would much rather have you get some sleep, since you have been so busy all day. I am going to have Morgan and his kids take over the night shift since they have been asleep since y'all left the ghost town." Rory didn't like this one bit, but instead of saying anything he just played with his whiskers, which he does when he runs out of food to eat.

"Jojo, thank you for all that you have done today. Ester is going to take over the evening shift." Ester, the strait-laced eastern screech owl, looked at Jojo and nodded her head. She had great respect for Jojo.

Lily continued, "William has already taken Ester to where the moonshine man lives, so she will lead the way this evening. Here is the lineup for this evening. Ester is in charge; the broadcaster barn owls will take over the communication, and will be stationed at all the different locations. Funk the skunk, Morgan, with his kids, and the flying squirrels, known as the Golden Gliders, will go to the moonshine man's house. William recruited Opal, the possum, who lives near the moonshine man's house. She is waiting for you all. Gretchen, our dependable great horned owl, will be stationed here at the command center; she will wake me for anything important. The passenger train has stopped for the night, so everyone can safely cross the bridge over the river. I hope we can get Dot in time to cross the bridge to our side before the sunrise train starts, if not we'll work out a plan."

"Okay, let's go get Dot!", cheered Abby.

54 * The Mean Moonshine Man * Gets his Prize

Jimbo was thrilled that finding Dot had been so easy, although he couldn't get over the weird behavior of the birds and that stupid squirrel. He pulled up to his shack, where his family had lived in for generations. He was the last surviving member. His two older brothers, who had been his best friends, had both been killed in the war, his momma had died giving birth to him, and his pappa died in prison, while serving time for selling moonshine.

Life just hadn't been fair to him, which made him sad, then mad. This made him hate them fancy city folks who were moving up to his neck of the woods. They seemed to have everything. He just despised them, with their fancy college degrees, cars, homes, restaurant dinners that cost an arm and a leg, plus drinking that stupid fancy grape juice they called wine, instead of buying his moonshine. They have their noses so high in the air they could drown in a rainstorm.

He was happy to be on his own land far away from everyone. As he parked his truck, he looked at Dot, who was curled up with Betty on the front seat. Dot just kept looking at him with her big black eyes. He could've sworn that her eyes looked sad, but his pappa had always said dogs didn't have feelings. He was never quite sure if his pappa was right about that.

He said, "Betty, git out'a the truck", and then he slammed the truck door in Dot's face. Jimbo took Betty to the musty old doghouse; it was a miracle it was still standing. "Here, girl, you are home now," he said as he clipped the chain to her collar.

Betty followed his orders, but she hated being stuck outside, especially now, as the winter was getting colder. She just wished she could go inside with him, especially at nighttime.

Jimbo went into his old shed to find some-thing that he could use to tie Dot up to the tree. He found an old rope and went to the truck to open the door. Dot had been watching his every move as she stared out the window. He took the rope, tied it around her neck with a tight knot, and dragged her out of the truck. He looked around to see if he should tie her to a different tree or the same one as Betty. Finally, he decided to tie her up on the same tree so maybe they could both squeeze in the dog-house together, as Dot was shaking from the cold already.

"Don't worry girl, I recon your family will be willing to pay a lot of money for you, so you should be home in two flicks of a kitty's tail.", he said as he walked away.

Once inside his shack, he started a fire in the ancient wood-burning stove. He remembered he should feed Betty, since she hadn't gotten her lunch that day, due to the stupid kids on the ATV. He scooped up a cup of cheap, dry, dog food and threw it out for both Betty and Dot.

Dot watched as Betty started gulping down the food, then took a bite herself. She immediately spit it out, it tasted awful. Cautiously she picked the icky nugget back up again and attempted to chew; she was so hungry. She managed to eat about six pieces, but then she just gave up; it was just too gross.

After Betty finished all the food she could reach, she went into her doghouse and bayed for Dot to join her. Dot crawled inside. Boy, did it stink, but she was happy to have the warmth of Betty next to her. After Dot was settled, Betty took in all the smells that were all over Dot. She smelled Burfoot, the catfish, a hint of Ruth, Rory, Morgan, and Morgan's kids. She had never had a friend to snuggle up with before; it made her smile.

Inside, Jimbo was writing out his ransom note.

Dear Owner of Dot

I have Dot and she is safe.
I will be happy to return Dot
to you but only for the amount
of 15,000 in cash bills. The
bills need to be old so they
can't be traced.

I will call you at 2pm to
tell you where to drop
the money. No COPS!
Once I get the money I will
tell you where you can pickup
Dot. Again No Cops

Jimbo got a rock that fit in his hand, wrapped the ransom note around it, and secured the note with a piece of twine. He laughed at the thought of "delivering the note" through their window. He looked at his clock and, seeing it was only 6:30 pm, he decided to take a nap since it had been such a long crazy day. He wanted to wait until midnight to deliver the note.

55 * The Night Shift Critters * On the Move

Ester, the screech owl, and the Broadcaster barn owls were soaring above the passenger train bridge on a beautiful clear night. Funk the skunk with Morgan's family were running along the tracks. The Golden Gliders were climbing up on the steel beams of the bridge, then gliding down to the rails, and then climbing back up again, to repeat the process. It was an extra thrill for them to be gliding above this wide river; they felt like they had a bit more wind to work with.

The night crew was making great time and, before they knew it, they were at the edge of the mean moonshine man's property. Ester let out her trilling hoot to alert Opal, the opossum, that they were there. Opal, was hanging out in a hollow tree to stay warm while she waited. She excitedly joined the night crew to tell them, all was calm, and everyone was sleeping.

Opal said, "Hey everyone, it's so nice to

meet you all. I am very excited to help. I've heard so many wonderful stories about all the cool things that you do, and I hope you don't mind, but I invited my friend and neighbor Benny."

Benny, a young black bear, popped out from behind the tree, smiling like crazy.

Benny said, "Hey y'all, what an honor to meet you. Opal and I love to chitchat, and we talk about y'all a lot. Right Opal?"

"Yes." Opal replied smiling.

"Why are you not hibernating right now?", Abby asked. She was always very inquisitive.

Benny said, "I know! Right? All the bears I know are hibernating right now. I was thinking about heading to my hideaway today. However, when your friend, William, the crow, showed up and asked Opal to help, I just couldn't miss this opportunity to be involved in this adventure, because y'all are legends in these woods."

"Where are you going to stay this winter?", Abby continued.

Benny laughed and said, "Promise not to tell?" Everyone looked at him and nodded. He laughed again and said, "Under the moonshine man's shack.".

"Okay everyone, let's get back to business.", Opal interjected. "I want to share a few things with you. The moonshine man is always coming out of his house at night, scared he heard something. I think he is scared someone is either going to steal his moonshine, or he is worried the cops are going to drive up. So, I think we need a plan in place in case he comes out this evening while we try to rescue Dot.

Everyone nodded in agreement.

Opal said, "Dot has a rope tied around her

neck. We can either untie it or cut it somehow."

All of Morgan's kids smiled, and nodded their heads, knowing they could take care of that rope lickety-split just like they had taken care of the bell rope. Morgan lifted his head in pride knowing this fact too.

Opal continued, "If you want to take Betty as well, she has a metal clasp that is connected to her collar; that should be easily opened with your nimble paws.", she said, looking at the raccoons. Everyone just looked at Opal with wide eyes, as they had never thought about taking another dog.

"Okay, okay. I know what you are thinking, but sweet Betty just doesn't have a great life. I have always fantasized about a better life for her. I tell you what, why don't you ask her."

They all mumbled in agreement. "Alright everyone, let's come up with our plan.", Opal ordered as she looked at Ester, who nodded.

56 * The Humans * Bedtime

Hazel was ready for bed; her heels were all bandaged up, after having been cleaned and covered with a thick layer of ointment.

"Dad, you know how you're always telling me to be quiet and settle down before bed? Well Dot and I just loved to play around, and I hope we can get her back so we can continue our play. I always went to bed happy with her."

Trying to sound reassuring, her dad said, "She made the whole family happy, and I'm confident we will get her back. For now, just close your eyes, and I'll read to you to help you fall asleep, okay?", Hazel nodded and closed her eyes.

Boris was staring out the window, which was very close to the large oak tree that Barney and the crows were hanging out in. He noticed some more action going on tonight. There were a few barn owls flying around, and one was chatting with Barney.

It made Boris happy to think that, with all this action, Dot had to be okay. He jumped down from the windowsill and hopped up on the bed and laid down next to Hazel. She petted him lightly as she was falling asleep. Boris started purring, then put his paw, reassuringly, on her shoulder, as they both fell asleep.

The Colonel softly closed the book when he heard Hazel's steady, deep breathing. He smiled as he shut off the lights and left the room.

57 * The Night Crew *

The night crew had their plan in place. They knew what to do and how to do it. Their

first task was to quietly wake Dot and Betty. Ester decided to send Abby in, since she already knew Dot. Abby crept to the doghouse under the bright stars of this dark night, being as stealthy as possible.

Once she reached the doghouse, she started to say Dot's name very softly, "Dot, please don't bark; it's me, Abby." Both dogs started waking up with dreams still fresh. Of course, Betty didn't know Abby, but she felt Dot's body shake with excitement. Betty relaxed and didn't let out her normal loud alarm bark.

"Here's the deal Dot, we're here to rescue you and get you back home."

Looking at Betty, Abby continued, "Betty, your possum friend, Opal, told us that you don't have a great life, so we wanted to ask you if you want to be rescued too. Do you?"

Betty was so surprised by all this that it was overwhelming for her. On the one hand, it was great having a friend in the doghouse with her, because she was always so lonely. On the other hand, being asked to decide if she wanted to leave the only home, she had ever known was a lot to take in. Yes, she had always dreamed about a nice warm home, but she kind of worried about the moonshine man, since she was his only companion, strange as it was. "Can I think about it?" Betty questioned.

"Absolutely. Our first task is to set up a few booby traps for the moonshine man, in case he comes out. Second, once we get the traps in place, we're going to start working on getting Dot's rope off her neck. Betty you will need to let us your decision then. Got it?", Abby finished

58 * The Moonshine Man *
Around Midnight

Jimbo had been checking the clock anxiously, eager to leave the house; as soon as his granddaddy's cuckoo clock struck midnight, he jumped up and grabbed his keys, hat, and the rock that was wrapped in the ransom note.

Abby and a few of her siblings were busily taking turns nibbling the rope around Dot's neck, since they could not undo the knot with their paws. Ester was watching from above, Opal from under the house, and the rest were hidden in the shadows. Everyone was anxiously waiting for Dot to be free of the rope and on alert in case the moonshine man came out of his house.

Jimbo opened the door and stepped down the stairs, but as soon as his feet hit the ground, they started sliding out into a side split; he managed to get them back together but, then they slid out to the front and the back of him. His legs were out of control.

The critters had placed thousands of acorns at the bottom of the steps. Losing his balance, Jimbo fell, landing in a huge pile of steaming, hot, bear poop, that Benny had been more than happy to contribute. The moonshine man started cussing up a storm, "Tater tots, fried green tomatoes, hoppin' Johns, what the heck is going on here?" He looked at the ransom note tied around the rock, now dripping with fresh, sloppy, brown poo. As he was staring at the brown gooey mess, something started pelting him. Jimbo looked up to see a whole gang of flying squirrels throwing acorns at him. He covered his head with his arms, causing him to get bear number two all over his face and head

"Hot fudge Sunday", he yelled, as he started to gag due to the bear poop. Then he noticed something coming up next to him; when he turned to look, he realized it was a skunk. Jimbo let out a loud panicked cry; he tried to get up to run, but those darn acorns were acting like marbles, and he just couldn't get on his two feet for the life of himself. Funk turned so his behind was facing the moonshine man, lifted his tail, and released an explosive squirt of skunk bomb liquid, right into Jimbo's eyes and gaping mouth.

Any sleeping critter, within a five-mile radius, could hear the piercing scream of the moonshine man. Jimbo upchucked his supper all over the acorns and his lap.

The prim and proper, Ester, let out a "Oh, oh, oh my." hoot, and then turned her head 180 degrees, so she didn't have to witness the vile scene below, caused by the booby-traps.

Jimbo was lying on the ground, rocking back and forth, for ten minutes. Finally, he managed to grab hold of the bottom step by his door, then the second step, and slowly managed to drag himself back into his shack. He was shouting the names of every food he could think of at the top of his lungs.

As soon as Jimbo was inside, Abby gleefully looked at Dot, who was now free of her rope. Dot jumped out of the doghouse and immediately wiggled on her back in the pine straw as a celebration of being free and to get rid of the mold smell.

"Well?", Abby looked at Betty.

"I don't know what will happen, but I wouldn't mind a bit of freedom, even if it is just a short bit of time.", Betty said, looking at Abby and the raccoon siblings who were crammed inside the doghouse.

Abby said, "Okay", and quickly used her nimble raccoon paws to open the latch, freeing Betty from her heavy chain.

Betty stood up with a big smile and said, "I've always hated that chain."

Abby came out of the doghouse and gave a thumbs up to Ester. The owl nodded her head and pointed her right wing back toward the way they had come from. Each critter tiptoed past the shack to the small trail, leaving the moonshine man behind.

59 * The Moonshine Man * Bear Poo and Skunk Juice

After crawling into his home, Jimbo got up and went to the sink to try to wash the stink off his face, rinsing his eyes. He unscrewed the cap on the tooth paste and filled his mouth full. He looked at himself in the dirty dull mirror.
He saw bloodshot eyes, his reddened nose dripping with snot, bubbling toothpaste foam dripping down his chin and bear poo was matted in his hair and streaked his face. It wasn't pretty.

"Where the heck did them flying squirrels and acorns come from?", he shouted as he spit out the toothpaste, which was flying everywhere. "It just don't make no sense. Nope, none at all. I don't even have one oak tree on this here property; papa cut them all down to build our old shed. Where the heck did they come from? I have lived here all my life and never seen a flying squirrel. There must've been fifty of them."

He'd always had bad luck, but this was ridiculous. He just shook his head and wiped a small tear forming at the corner of his eye. Not wanting to feel any sad emotions, he started cussing again, while changing his threadbare overalls to an even older pair of overalls that had holes everywhere.

He rewrote the ransom note, but this time he put the note in an old moonshine mason jar.

Jimbo opened the door and looked at all the acorns lying there, shaking his head in bafflement. He stepped off the side of the stairs and carefully made his way around the acorns to his truck. Normally, he would've taken Betty, but he was feeling so low that he just didn't have the energy to bring her along.

Jimbo headed straight to Dot's house then drove around the block a few times on the lookout for anyone still up or maybe someone walking a dog. He parked his truck at the corner. Still reeking of skunk, the moonshine man was getting out of the truck when he noticed quite a few barn owls flying over his truck and by Dot's house. Weird, he thought, as he walked quickly to the house.

Standing on the sidewalk, he looked at the house and tried to figure out which window to throw the mason jar through. He figured the big window would be best. Jimbo walked halfway into the yard and threw the jar, busting the top few panes of the bay window.

Jumping from the loud noise, Jimbo turned and ran as fast as he could to his truck, which he had left running, to make sure he could make a quick getaway.

60 * The Humans *
Strange Noises

The Colonel and his wife woke up to the sound of glass breaking. "Stay right here.", he said. Putting on his slippers and robe, he picked up his phone, noticed the time was 12:45 am, he turned on the phone's flashlight.

First, he stopped by the twins' bedroom and went to Hazel's room, relieved to see all the kids sleeping.

Going down the stairs, he saw movement. The Colonel stopped moving but then he realized it was Boris, he released a deep breath.

Boris was trying to shake off the glass that landed on him as he slept at his favorite spot. Plus, ever since Dot disappeared, Boris wanted to be close to the front door if Dot came home.

The Colonel picked up Boris and took him to the kitchen to get a good look at him. He got Dot's brush to carefully remove the glass. "No blood, Boris. That's great, I think you will be okay.", the Colonel announced, as Boris rubbed his creek on the Colonel's hand.

"Okay, let's see what broke that window."

As they both headed towards the bay

window, they saw a mixture of broken clear glass from the window and some broken pale blue glass as well. "That is weird.", the Colonel said to Boris.

"Meooow", Boris said loudly, and walked to the note that the Colonel hadn't seen.

"Oh, thank you Boris.", the Colonel said as he picked up the note. Boris just stared at him, as he did that silent thing they call 'reading', to figure out what was on the paper.

"Fifteen thousand dollars!", the Colonel exclaimed under his breath, trying not to wake the family. He went to the couch and sat down, patting next to him so Boris would jump up. "Well, the note said not to call the police, but that is the first thing we are going to do in the morning. The good news is that Dot is alive; the bad news is that some jerk has her. Alright, Boris, let's get some sleep and we will work on getting our girl back tomorrow. But first, I need to clean up all this broken glass."

Boris fell asleep, curled up on the couch, as the Colonel cleaned up the glass, so none of his family would hurt themselves in the morning. However, he made sure to save all the larger pieces of the blue glass.

As soon as the Colonel left the room, Boris jumped up on the table to look out at Barney. The barred owl was so happy to see that Boris looked okay that he leapt off his branch and soared by the window in a celebratory flight. He had been very worried about his new friend, getting hurt from the glass. They both looked each other in the eyes and smiled in their own special ways.

61 * The Command Center *
Deep In the Night

The Broadcasters were having a busy night following the moonshine man and the critters, all while flying back and forth reporting to Gretchen. Gretchen, the great horned owl, who loved her large, tufted ears. She was always excited to get the latest updates from the Broadcasters so she could share them with Lily when she woke up in the morning.

Gretchen was the polar opposite of her best friend Ester, who was very prim and proper. All the barn owls, with their cute heart shaped faces, always joke that Gretchen was big, bold, and brassy. Gretchen always let out a loud hoot when she heard this. She loved it and agreed completely.

She was happy with the reports she was getting about Dot's rescue, but she was a bit concerned about the cat that was sleeping by the window. Her other concern was that daylight would be here faster than you knew it, and she didn't think it would be smart for the critters to go over the train bridge so close to dawn.

The tourist train left the home station around 5 am to pick up folks in town for the sunrise tour.

"Please tell Ester that I am a bit worried about the train", she directed Venus, a barn owl. Venus nodded with a long, slow blink as she took off into the clear, dark sky.

62 * The Moonshine Man *
Finding an Empty Doghouse

"What the heck!", the moonshine man yelled, as he pulled up to his yard with his headlight shining into the doghouse. He couldn't see Betty or Dot. He parked his truck, leaving the headlights on so he could inspect the doghouse up close.

"Chicken gizzards!", he yelled as he picked up Dot's frayed rope.

Then the "international cursing" began. This is what he did when he was SUPER MAD.

"Burritos, tacos, guacamole, refried beans, and dag-nab salsa." He yelled at the top of his lungs. He paced back and forth, in and out of the light beams, as both Opal and Benny watched the man from underneath his shack. They looked at each other, backing further away from the man having a massive hissy fit.

After the moonshine man went into his home, the entire shack shook as he was stomping around. Opal and Benny looked at each other, wondering if they should move from under the shack, as they continued to hear him still cussing inside, slamming things around as he yelled, "What the heck am I going to do now?", followed by another loud scream, and then nothing.

"Silence", Opal whispered to Benny. They

were grateful because they were both very tired after a fun evening of rescuing Dot and Betty, plus pranking the moonshine man. Although, inside, they kind of felt a tiny bit bad for the mean moonshine man.

63 * The Critters *
Middle Of the Night

Ester was leading the way with the original crew after they said goodbye and thank you to Opal and Benny. She was aware of the time and, when Venus, the barn owl, flew to relay what Gretchen had said, she knew she needed to come up with a new way to get all the critters over the river at dawn. She had an idea, so she sent Venus to get some of the Broadcasters to recruit as many river otters as they could find and tell them all to go to the base of the train bridge.

Ester knew that her night crew was getting exhausted, so she was not pushing them to go as fast as she wanted. She knew mistakes happened when everyone was tired; she definitely didn't want any mishaps, especially when she learned of Burfoot falling into the well. Ester also didn't trust going over the train bridge once the train started its sunrise run. She knew the raccoons and flying squirrels could climb the beams of the bridge, but Dot and Betty just wouldn't be able to. "Better safe than sorry.", she said to the wind, as she soared above the treetops with a sharp eye on her friends below.

"I am so tired, can we rest just a little bit?", Abby said as she looked at her dad.

Relieved he said, "Yes, that's fine, it's been a long journey.", since he too was tuckered out.

Ester flew down and let everyone know it was okay to rest and that she was working on a plan to get over the river, so they didn't have to rush anymore.

They were happy for a break but then they all froze in place. They looked at each other as they heard the howling and yapping of a huge pack of coyotes. The critter's hair rose on their backs.

There had been coyotes in the mountains since the 1970s, but a new pack had recently moved in and the rumor was, they were not friendly. After about ten minutes, the howling stopped, and the good news was they seemed far away.

Dot, Betty, Funk the skunk, Morgan, and his kids gathered together to take a cat nap. The Flying Headbangers climbed up a tree rich with fungus growing on it and they started chowing down for an early morning snack.

Ester surveyed the crew and was grateful for the moment of calm, which she knew the critters needed before they continued.

64 * The Night Critters * Twilight

As they approached the river, Dot was excited seeing the sun rise over the trees and all the beautiful Broadcasters hanging out on the bridge. Then she noticed these funny animals that had faces and whiskers kind of like her own. A whole group of the animals were climbing up the muddy riverbank, then sliding down the mud and back into the water. It looked like they were having a blast.

Ester flew back and forth trying to count the otters the Broadcaster summoned.

She said, "Venus, please tell Gretchen and Lily to have the day crew to meet us on their side of the river within an hour or so. Ground crew, rest, eat, or whatever you want to do while I figure out our next plan."

Ester flew up into a tall pine tree to think. She had been hoping for more otters; now, she needed to figure out what she was going to do with her limited resources.

65 * The Night Critters *
Sunrise

Ester landed on a rock next to the otters and her crew. "Gather around, we have a few options. Otters, I have gathered you here this morning to ask you to band together to create furry rafts that can carry Dot and all her friends over the river. I know that, as river otters, you don't normally make rafts, like your cousins, the sea otters, but I hope you can accommodate us. The Headbangers fly and flying squirrels can climb on the bridge and glide over the river. I was hoping more otters could make it here, but I think fourteen of you are enough. I see a log over there." Ester said, pointing her wing to the log, which was covered with a group of large and small turtles basking in the new light of day. Everyone turned their heads and observed the log covered with turtles on the riverbank.

"If we can pry the log out of the muck into the water, we can get Funk and Morgan and his family on it, and four of the otters can direct it. Two otters in the front and two in the rear.
If we can get three of you otters on your backs, holding your paws together to make a raft, Dot can lay on your bellies. The same thing with Betty, but we would need at least six otters, and one extra otter could swim around to make sure everyone is doing okay."

Olly, the eldest otter said, "This sounds like a blast and easy to do.", looking at all his friends and family who all nodded their heads.

The mission to cross the river on the living rafts was officially on.

66 * The Humans * Calling The Police

Rising early, the first thing the Colonel did was call the police to report the ransom demand for Dot's return. Soon after, the cops were knocking on the door.

Greetings were exchanged and the sheriff said, "Just call me Sheriff, like everyone else does, and this is my deputy, Peter."

The Colonel led them to the kitchen table, saying, "Please have a seat. Would you like some coffee?", he offered.

"No thanks.", both men responded.

"What can we do for you this morning?", the sheriff asked.

The Colonel put two pieces of paper on the table. First, the flyer with the reward for Dot and second, the paper that the moonshine man had thrown into the house the night before.

Both men looked at the papers and Peter picked up the ransom note, after pulling on a pair of latex gloves.

"I feel like I have seen this handwriting before", Peter stated, after studying the note.

"What's going on?" All the men looked up to see Hazel standing there in her Boston terrier pajamas. They were silent. "Daddy, what's going

on? If this is about Dot, you need to tell me."
Hazel demanded.

The Colonel nodded and tapped the seat
next to him. "Come, sit down and I will explain."
He repeated the same story to Hazel that he had
just told the police. "May I see the note they threw
through the window?", Hazel asked.

The sheriff handed Hazel some latex
gloves to put on that were way too big for her, but
they would keep the note free of her fingerprints.
"This paper kind of stinks like a skunk. Some of
the letters are backwards just like the firewood
man's letters are backward on his red truck.", she
stated.

Peter looked at Hazel very seriously.
"That's it. She's right. I knew these letters looked
familiar. I went to school with Jimmy Johnson my
whole life, and all the different teachers we had
could never get Jimmy to print the letters 'S' and
'R' correctly. By George, this girl is a genius."
Peter let out a big, loud, belly laugh and said,
"Oh, poor Jimmy. He's had a very sad life. He
used to be so much fun when he was young. The
cutest little blond kid. He was the class clown,
everyone loved him, including the teachers. He
got in so much trouble from his grandma once
when he said a cuss word that I never heard him
use a cuss word again. He would scream out
names of food when he was mad. We all thought
it was so funny, but we never let him hear us
laugh."

Peter suddenly became deep in thought,
but finally continued, "When he lost both his
brothers in the war and his daddy he changed.
Sheriff, you're new to town, but one of the ways
his family made money has always been a very
well-known secret. The family has been making

106

moonshine for generations. Jimbo drives around in his old truck selling firewood, but the folks that grew up here all know that he's also selling his moonshine. After Jimmy's dad died in prison everyone just felt it was best to just 'look the other way' and let him keep on with his family tradition."

Again, Peter paused. "It's so sad. I can't believe he would do something as stupid as this. I wish we hadn't lost touch; but with my job as a cop, I guess it was complicated."

The sheriff saw that Peter had completed his thoughts and added, "I just met him the other day in the drug store parking lot. I was admiring his beautiful bloodhound. Well, let's see if we can get some firm evidence and then we will go to his house."

The sheriff then directed his attention to the Colonel, "Can you please let me look at the blue glass you picked up last night, there might be a piece that we can get a fingerprint from. Also, can you ask your neighbors if they might have any surveillance video." The sheriff looked at his partner, "I assume you know where Mr. Johnson lives."

"Yep." Peter replied, with a sad heart.

"I remember seeing his dog, too, Sheriff.", Hazel piped in. "I felt bad the puppy was in the back of the truck, especially in this cold weather."

The sheriff nodded his head and gave her a smile, but his eyes were sad.

67 * The Night Critters * Rising Sun

Ester and all the others watched as Olly explained to the turtles how they would like to borrow the log to get their new friends over the river. The turtles bobbled their heads side to side in agreement, if they got their log back afterwards. Olly agreed they would use all their otter power to bring the log back upstream for them. The turtles bobbled their heads again, then slipped into the water to get out of the critters' way.

Within minutes, all the raccoons, Funk the skunk, the otters, Dot, and Betty were covered in mud trying to push the long log into the river. They had been loosening the wood for about 20 minutes and most likely would've given up, had it not been for the otters being so entertaining. The otters were being overly dramatic with their pushing and pulling, then climbing on the log and sliding off, that even Ester from up above couldn't help from hooting with laugher.

The log was starting to shift, when suddenly, a loud, sucking, popping boom sounded, the bond between the log and the mud broke loose. It was gratifying to finally see this massive chunk of wood slide into the river.

Everyone let out a roar of laugher, celebrating, and the otters happily jumped into the river to take control of this soon-to-be long raft. The raccoons jumped on the log, which immediately rolled over dumping them in the water. All the raccoon eyes were wide open as their heads popped out of the chilly water, chattering as they swam to the muddy bank.

Ester flew down to the riverbank, trying very hard not to get any mud on her. She tiptoed to a branch stuck in the mud and climbed on top of it, once she knew it was stable, announced, "My friends, you need to be very careful when you're transporting everyone across the river. The river is fast flowing with many rocks, I do not want anyone to get hurt. I love your pranks and how funny you are, but we secure the log, so it won't twist in the water. Those of you carrying Dot and Betty also need to take this very seriously. The river is very cold. Dot and Betty would not do well in these temperatures."

Olly smiled at Ester and the rest of the crew saying, "Oh yes, we will take this very seriously, and we will do it with joy. We respect your opinion and understand how serious this mission is. No need to worry"

Ester said, "Wonderful. Everyone let's get going. I'm ready to get you all over the river so our night crew can get some sleep", while covering her beak with a wing to suppress a yawn.

The otters jumped into position. Three otters turned on their backs, held their paws together, and looked at Dot, smiling. Dot, who loved water but hated being cold, slowly walked over to her personal raft, who were now happily humming. She stepped on their floating bodies, and they all sank a little bit. When she was fully on all three of them, she laid down, resting her chin on her paws. Olly nudged them off the edge of the bank and into the river. The two otters who were on the outside of this three-otter raft used their free paws and tails to navigate the flowing currents as they headed to the opposite bank.

Betty watched Dot as she safely floated away, giving her the courage to step onto her own personal otter raft.

Olly launched Betty and the larger otter raft off the shore and then did the same with Funk the skunk, and the raccoon family on the long log. Funk was at the very back. The two otters, who were navigating the back of the log, looked at each other, then up at Funk. The otters gave Funk a smile, but moved closer to Morgan, fearing of accidentally getting sprayed by Funk. Again, they smiled at Funk grateful that he didn't notice their fear of his pungent spray.

With everyone safely on the river, Olly looked at Ester and smiled, as he pushed himself off on his back. He clapped his fronts paws together, then raised them, as if he were creating a "V" for victory. Ester trusted him and raised her wings to create her own 'V'.

Ester flew up among the Broadcasters and the crows, who were circling above the land critters, when she heard the honking of geese above. The geese, who were heading south late in the season, saw all the commotion below and decided it would be a good time to rest. Splashing down and honking greetings as they joined this unusual mix.

68 * The Passenger Train *

Five young cousins were on the train as it went over the wide river, when they saw this strange assembly of otters, raccoons, geese, and dogs floating down the river. Immediately, they started yelling at their parents, who were busy talking on the other side of the train aisle.

One young mother said, "Yes, yes, it's very exciting riding this train, but we're talking right now, so please try to be a bit quieter".

All the kids had heard this a million times before and knew their parents wouldn't look, so they quit vying for their attention and turned back to watch the aquatic parade with amazement.

The train conductor also saw what was happening below on the river, but he just rubbed his eyes, saying to himself, "I really need to get some glasses.", shaking his head and rubbing his eyes again.

69 * The Critters *
Crossing the River

For the first few minutes floating on the otter raft, Dot was terrified, but she was doing her best to conceal her fear. She lay as low as she could but slowly, she lifted her head to look

111

around. The river was fast, and some water had gotten Dot's feet wet, but they were warmed by the otter's thick fur. The otters, picking up on Dot's fear, let out reassuring clicking noises, while using their tails to turn the raft around, so Dot could see the rest of her friends.

Betty's otter raft paddled a bit faster so they could be closer to Dot. Betty was lifting her nose taking in all the wonderful river smells, as the wind blew her ears back flapping away. It was so magical to her that she bayed out a loud bloodhound 'Ah-Rooooh'. The otters, hearing Betty's joyous howl all let out an even louder chorus of trilling, chirping, and clicking vocalizations.

Olly was darting under the floating log and popping up in front of, or behind, Dot and Betty, with a big smile on his face, and bursting out with, "Surprise!". Each time he did this, the geese would lift their beaks to the sky and let out a series of honks. The swimming geese formed a "V", pointing to the opposite riverbank where the day crew was waiting.

Rory was nervously pacing back and forth, eating nuts, worms, anything he could find. Earlier, Dot had told Rory that she was not a big fan of fish, because of all the bones. Being a food connoisseur, Rory shared a few ideas with the bald eagle on how to score 'people food' from town and campsites. So, in addition to being anxious about the river crossing, he was excited to see what the eagle might drop off for the two dogs.

Rusty, the fox, was watching the crossing stoically, on the river's bank. Rose was goofing around with Burfoot, Jeremy, and the rest of the Scurriers, to escape the boredom of waiting.

Ruth was resting on a branch above the river. Her feathered chest was puffed up, full of pride for her friend Ester and her brilliant plan to cross the river.

All the different woodpeckers were hammering away at the same time, on different trees, like a drum circle, to celebrate the arrival of their furry friends. The mood was festive after the scare they had the day before, with the close call with the train and the pup-napping by the moonshine man.

70 * The Mean Moonshine Man * Defeated

Jimbo woke up feeling defeated. His dog Betty, the Boston terrier, and the ransom money he was counting on, were all long gone. Losing the ransom money meant he had lost his dream of buying the newer truck he had seen for sale downtown. He had lost a whole bunch of money during the wreck when all his jars of moonshine were broken. He didn't have a spare tire anymore, and he still reeked of skunk funk.

He was just too tired to be mad.

He made his morning coffee and looked out his kitchen window at the empty doghouse. "I just don't know what the heck has been going on. I have lived in these hills all my life, and I've never seen so many critters and birds like I've seen in the past two days", he said, talking to his lonesome self.

"There must be something in the water. Either that, or aliens have come down from the heavens and taken possession of these here critters. I need to ask some other folks in town if they've noticed this weird behavior from any animals. Or am I just losing my mind and going batty?"

The moonshine man shook his head and grabbed a broom to sweep away the acorns that had mysteriously appeared by his back steps. Sweeping the acorns, he observed the smashed-down pile of bear poop and shuddered with that memory. He had never seen a bear on his property before, most likely because he always had dogs. He would be surprised to know that bears had been hibernating under his shack for years.

Jimbo walked to the doghouse to get a good look at the frayed rope and the latch that he used to connect Betty to the chain. The fray on the rope didn't look like it had been cut by a knife or a pair of scissors. Each tiny thread was cut at a slightly different length, like how a mouse or some other animal would nibble away, fiber by fiber.

Who, or what, had taken the dogs, was all he could think about. Are the dogs, okay? His heart started to hurt a bit. A broken heart was something he had worked really hard not to feel, since he had lost his family. But now, he was sad that Betty was gone. Then, he was thinking about the family that was looking for Dot; they must feel the same way. That was another thing he tried not to do, to think about how others feel; but now, he couldn't stop. Jimbo felt like a balloon after a party. He was 100% deflated. All his plans for the day had evaporated, and his dream of a new truck were gone, too. He had never felt so lonely in his whole life.

71 * The Sheriff *
A Tip

The sheriff and his deputy had gotten a tip from a tourist. She thought she had seen a man carrying the lost Boston terrier that was posted on the flyers around town. She had called the number on the flyer, and the Colonel had asked her to call the Sheriff.

"Hey. My name is Georgia. Yesterday I was sitting outside the drug store, looking at a map of the Appalachian Trail. I saw all these crows going crazy above the parking lot by the AT approach trail. Then I saw an old man running with a black and white dog in his arms and a bloodhound on a leash. A bunch of crows were circling above his red truck, as if they wanted to attack. They were making forceful squawking noises. And even crazier; some of the crows seemed like they were following the truck as it pulled away. I've never seen anything like it. Never. I think something might've been written on the truck, but I really couldn't take my eyes off the crows. I hope you don't think I'm nuts!"

The sheriff laughed, reassuringly, to the sweet woman that had called his office, "Ma'am, I never think anyone is crazy that has a good tip. Who knows what was going on with the crows. The good news is you are helping with a missing dog case that has now become a crime. I call that very courageous. Do you remember what time of day it was?"

"Oh, it must've been about 2:30 or 3 pm, sometime around there."

"And this was definitely yesterday?", the sheriff continued.

"Oh, yes sir. I had just pulled into town from Atlanta."

"Welcome, Ms. Georgia, we are glad you are here to visit. And, if you don't mind, could you please give me all your contact information? Also, how long will you be in town? We may need you to identify the man in the red truck."

"I will be here for the next few days; there is so much I want to do". Then she continued with where she was staying, and all the rest of her contact information.

The sheriff hung up and looked at Peter. "Let's go to the drug store and ask Mr. Moore if we can look at his surveillance tapes."

72 * The Critters *
Reaching the Riverbank

As the sun lifted to the sky glowing a mixture of reds, purples, and oranges, the daytime critters had stopped what they were doing to watch, as Dot and the others approached the riverbank.

Rory was the only one not watching; he was eyeing the sky, waiting to see what the bald eagle might bring. He was tapping his little paw fingers together chanting, "Food, food, food, please be quick to bring us food."

Jojo was so happy to see Dot that he flew down and landed on Dot's head as the otter rafts were approaching the shore. He greeted the three otters, happily cawing and flapping his wings to his inner beat. He was so grateful Dot was safe.

The second Dot hopped off the otter raft and landed on solid ground, all the Scurriers ran to Dot. They were running around her, on top of her, below her, and hugging her legs. Dot's body quivered for the joy of friendship.

Rusty and Rose both greeted Dot with a nose-to-nose touch. The crows all cawed, and the woodpeckers hammered away.

Ruth flew down and reached up to stroke Dot's whiskers with the tip of her wing.

Betty crawled off her raft of otters, soaking in all the celebratory vibes, letting out a very loud and happy bay. All the daytime critters stopped what they were doing to stare at Betty, shocked by her booming howl. Then they saw the joy she had shining from her eyes, the daytime critters welcomed her as well.

Within minutes, the rest of the otters and the night crew were all on the shore with the day crew. There was an overwhelming feeling of relief and happiness.

Rory hopped with excitement when he saw the bald eagle coming over the trees with something big in his talons. He sat up on his hind legs to try to get a better look. The eagle dropped two steaming hot ribeye steaks in front of the dogs. Rory ran over to smell the yummy goodness. His whiskers vibrated as he drooled with anticipation.

Rory then yelled up to the eagle, who was observing the crowd below, and asked, "Steak? Two steaks? In all my years in these woods I have never been so lucky to score a whole steak. How did you do it?"

The eagle lifted his head, proud of his new food challenge, "A group of men at the campground by town were making steak and eggs for breakfast", he shuddered at the thought of the men eating eggs. "The men had way too much food and I'm sure they will not miss it, but they sure were screaming at me as I flew away.", the eagle chuckled.

Betty's dream just came true, a whole steak, with a BONE! She let out a happy howl and started chowing down. Dot started eating her steak, too, but stopped to look up at Rory, who started peppering her with questions. "How is it, Dot? You know I told the eagle you didn't like fish bones, right, Dot? I have never had a steak like that, only fat left in the trash can. Does it taste as good as it looks, Dot? Do you think you will eat the whole thing, Dot?"

Dot looked at her friend and said, "How about we share?" She had steak leftovers at home all the time, so she wanted Rory to experience the goodness too.

"I don't mind if I do, thank you very much!", he said, gratefully, as he gave a double thumbs up to the eagle above.

Ester and Jojo met, so he could get the update about the night before and then share the plans going forward. "Lily wants us to go to her den to hang out today, and then she wants a limited crew to travel through the woods after sunset to escort Dot home. The big freeze is coming tonight, so it is very important to get her

118

home this evening. We will be traveling at night, so we don't have to worry about so many humans. After the man took Dot, Lily wants to be extra careful to protect her.", Jojo told Ester.

"Sounds like a good plan.", Ester agreed.

"May I have everyone's attention", Jojo sang out. Everyone looked at Ester and Jojo, who were both on a boulder by the water's edge.

With pride, Ester expressed, "I want to give my sincere gratitude and thanks to all the otters for safely getting everyone across the river."

"It was our total honor to help, and what a joy it was to start our day with so many new friends.", Olly said, as he took a deep bow. The other otters followed his lead, bowing in unison, and gave a loud cheer of otter chirping.

Ester continued, "I also want to thank the geese for their company and leading the way."

The geese let out multiple honks while flapping their wings and splashing the water.

"Jojo has just informed me that the day and night crews are to go to Lily's den and hang out today. We need to get Dot home this evening before the big freeze."

When she heard the word 'home', Dot did a few skips, while wagging her stubby tale and butt enthusiastically.

Jojo piped up, "Okay let's get back to Lily's. And once again, many thanks to everyone."

Dot went to the otters and gave each of them a tender nudge with her nose.

Winking at Dot, Olly said, "My new friend, anytime you want a ride in the river we will always be here for you. It looks like we could be family because we have the same cute whiskers."

Dot gave Olly another nudge, followed by a big, slurpy lick on his cheek.

After all the goodbyes, the otters joined together to push the log back into the water, to return it to the turtles.

The geese all did a little run on the water as they flapped their wings, honking as they lifted off, to heading to warmer weather for the winter.

The crows flew off in different directions to update Lily and Gretchen at Lily's den, plus the crows and Barney, stationed at Dot's house.

73 * The Sheriff and Deputy *
Mid-Morning

The Sheriff and Peter were sitting in the drugstore, waiting for Mr. Moore, the pharmacist, to arrive. They both rose when they saw him walk in.

"Morning, Mr. Moore. I heard you were doing a bit of fishing this morning from your salesclerk. Any luck?", the sheriff asked.

"No, but I am just happy to get a bit of fresh air and a touch of sun on a chilly morning before getting to work. What can I do for you, Sheriff?"

"We would like to see some of your surveillance footage of the parking lot from yesterday afternoon around 2:30, if you don't mind?"

"Is everything okay, Sheriff?"

"Someone took the lost Boston terrier and

120

is asking for a bunch of money. You have the flyer about the terrier on your door."

"Yep, sure do. That is an awful shame.", Mr Moore responded.

The sheriff continued, "We have a witness who believes she saw someone take the dog, so we want to follow up."

"Not a problem, I'll have my assistant help you. Jack, will you help the sheriff and Peter with what they need?", Mr. Moore called to his nephew.

Mr. Moore excused himself, as he stepped behind the pharmacy counter and put on his white coat.

Jack, who was much more computer-savvy than his uncle, had set up all the security cameras. Looking at the sheriff he asked, "Time and date please?"

After the sheriff responded, Jack typed away, and both the Sheriff and Peter saw images of the moonshine man going into the woods.

"This is who we are looking for", the sheriff told Jack.

Jack sped up the video, then he froze the frame on Jimbo, caught in the act of running over the train tracks towards his truck.

"There he is, plain as day, with the dog in his arms. We've got our man.", the sheriff said to his deputy.

"Keep rolling the video. Would you look at all the crows above him?", Peter commented.

"Never seen anything like it, that's for sure. Could you please print out a still of this image for me, Jack?", the sheriff asked.

"No problem, I'll have it in a jiffy", Jack said, as he left the back office.

"Wow, the crows", Peter repeated.

"You got that right", exclaimed the Sheriff.

74 * The Critters *
Before the Night's Adventure

Dot and Betty were lying on the ground outside Lily's den, still enjoying the bones from the steaks the bald eagle had dropped for them that morning; they had made sure to not leave them behind at the river. Rory was enjoying eating earth worms and hickory nuts. The Broadcasters, Ester, and Gretchen were sound asleep, in the trees surrounding Lily's den. Lily was sitting on the large boulder with Ruth and Jojo, just enjoying watching everyone. Lily said, "I have to say, this is the craziest mission we have ever had. Most are simple, but this has been over the top. I'm concerned that the humans are going to start noticing our behavior, especially that moonshine man." Giggling, she went on, "Oh, I love how creative everyone has been." she paused, then said, "Boy, oh boy. What a last couple of days. I'm glad we are all safe and sound."

Lily was silent and reflective as she watched the squirrels playing in a tree. She laughed and shook her head, watching the chipmunks challenging each other in a contest to see who could cram the most nuts in their cheeks. Looking up into the trees, she admired the sleeping owls and sweet flying squirrels.

As she continued talking with Ruth and

Jojo, she made sure to keep her voice low because she did not want to disturb Morgan and family, who were sleeping in Lily's den.

Softly, Lily continued, "I am going out on the mission tonight."

"What?", both Ruth and Jojo gasped, in surprise. They knew how secretive Lily was, and she was always so careful to avoid being spotted by humans.

"Quiet", Lily whispered, "I'm only going as far as the railroad tracks. I am very concerned about the new pack of coyotes. They seem to be aggressively looking for new territory. We would welcome them if they weren't so disagreeable and unfriendly. So, just to be on the safe side, I want to be there. I really wish that both of you could join us this evening, but nighttime just isn't your thing."

Jojo did a musical bob in agreement and Ruth let out a soft caw.

75 * The Sheriff *
After Lunch

Hanging up his cell phone, the sheriff looked at Peter, who was driving the police car to the moonshine man's house. "That was the Colonel. He said a couple of his neighbors' security cameras caught the moonshine man's truck around 12:45 last night, and their next-door neighbor's camera caught a grainy image of a man throwing the jar. The Colonel is going to text me some of the videos shortly."

Peter just shook his head, "Oh, this is a sad day for me. I really hate everything about this. I just wish I could get away with giving Jimmy a good old-fashioned scolding, I know he would listen. I also regret that I didn't stay close with him and invite him in with my family after he lost his pa; I knew he had to be lonely. If I had, maybe he wouldn't have done something as stupid as this."

Peter started driving a bit slower than the speed limit, but the sheriff didn't say anything because he could see his friend was suffering.

"I will be happy to do all the talking if you like. You don't think he will come out with a rifle or anything, do you?", the sheriff asked.

"No sir, even though the family made moonshine for generations, the kids were taught to always respect lawmen."

"Good to know", the sheriff sighed with relief.

Peter activated his turn signal. "Here we go. This road leads up to his home, and good thing it isn't raining." The dirt road was narrow and steep, with deep ruts, lots of bumps and no gravel.

"Oh, I agree. I bet this road is a slip-and-slide in the rain", the sheriff stated.

Minutes later, the sheriff didn't see why Peter was slowing down; he couldn't see any roads or driveways. Peter pulled into a tunnel of rhododendrons, a hardy evergreen bush that has showy flowers in the spring and summer.

"Wow, this is kind of cool", the Sheriff said in amazement.

"He likes his privacy, that's for sure", Peter agreed.

76 * The Moonshine Man *
Cop Car

Jimbo was sitting on the back of his truck, feeling blue. The spare tire he had used to fix the flat, after his run in with the yahoo boys on the ATV, had a slow leak. The threadbare tire now only held half the air it was supposed to.

He could hear a car approaching. "I don't like the sound of that, no siree bob", he muttered to himself. He quickly walked to the shed, that was on the opposite side of the yard, from his moonshine stills by the creek. Hiding, he peeked out to see who was coming.

"Ain't nobody been up this way in years. Years! Shoot, only a handful of folks even know about this place. I don't have a good feeling. Nope, nope, nope". He nervously chattered to himself.

As the cop car pulled into the yard, Jimbo's shoulders and head dropped. First, the sheriff got out. Then he saw his old buddy, Peter, get out.

"Fudgesicle", he swore.

"Jimmy Johnson!", the sheriff hollered.

"Jimbo!", Peter called out.

"Yep, I'm here. What can I do for you fellas today? Nice to see you again, Peter; been a minute or two", said Jimbo, trying to hide his nervousness.

"Yep, it's real good to see you too, Jimbo. I think of you often, and I regret we lost touch; we used to be so close growing up."

The men gathered around; the crows were perched in the trees above, watching and listening to everything.

"This is a bit awkward for me, since I know you two are old friends, but I am here to arrest you today", said the sheriff.

"Why?", asked Jimbo, He was thinking to himself, 'who ratted me out about my moonshine?' He didn't think they were there about the dog, at all, because he had told those city folks not to call the cops.

"Well, it's about that dog you took and then tried to get a ransom for. So, we are here today to take you in and to return the dog to the family."

Jimbo's knees almost gave out on him. "I don't have that dog.", Jimbo informed the two men.

"We have it all on video, including you throwing the jar through the window.", the sheriff stated.

"Well, you might have that stupid video of me, but that dog is gone and so is my Betty."

Peter and the sheriff looked at each other.

"There is the doghouse that is Betty's home, and that black and white dog was in there with Betty last night when I left to deliver the ransom note. Then, when I got back, they were gone. Both of them! Here, let me show you."

As they all walked to the doghouse, the sheriff cringed at the poor bloodhound's living conditions. He hated to see dogs chained up; it just felt so cruel to him. Jimbo held up the frayed rope, "See? It looks like small teeth nibbled their way through this here rope. And I have no idea who unlatched Betty's spring hook. It is just a mystery to me."

"Are you telling the truth, Jimbo?" Peter looked deeply at his friend of fifty years; he didn't think Jimbo would lie to him.

"Yep, unfortunately. A lot of strange things have been happening, and this is one of them. My luck has been in the dumps lately, and the critters, or some kind of aliens, have come to mess with me", Jimbo sincerely expressed to Peter.

Peter placed his hand on his old friend's shoulder and said, "I believe you Jimbo."

"Well, that little girl sure is going to be sad to hear you don't have her dog", said the Sheriff.

"Yes sir, I do believe you are right. I am embarrassed I acted so rash and did something so stupid. I guess I got real selfish. I just wanted a new truck. My old truck over there, who I call Bertha, is just old and sick. I barely have money for my monthly bills, much less for repairs or a new truck. Bertha has a real hard time just getting up the road sometimes.", continued Jimbo, hanging his head in shame.

Peter said with a bit of regret in his voice, "Oh, I wish I knew. My brother has a shop in the next town over, and we would've been happy to help you".

The sheriff asked Jimbo "Okay, is there anything you need to do before we take you in?".

"Well, let me turn off my lights and my coffee pot, then I'll lock up. I'll be right back.", Jimbo said, as he walked away with a cloud of gloom surrounding him.

After he left, Peter looked at the sheriff and said, "Thanks for not being too rough on him."

The sheriff didn't have anything to say, so he just nodded.

As the police car drove back through the tunnel of rhododendrons, two of the three crows took off. One went to update Lily, and the other to update Barney at the human's house. One crow stayed, just to keep an eye out.

77 * Boris and His Human Family *

Boris was sitting on his table, keeping an eye out for the crows' comings and goings. Any time he saw a crow wake up Barney to relay something, he would smash his face against the glass, as if that would let him hear what was being said. Each time the crow flew off, Barney would look at Boris and blink his eyes, letting Boris know everything was okay.

Anyway, that is what Boris believed, or wanted to believe.

Boris turned his attention to the Colonel, who had just ended a call with the sheriff and put his phone into the back pocket of his jeans. The family was spread out in the living room after finishing their lunch. The twins were having a tug of war with a doll. Hazel was flipping through a book but wasn't focusing on it. Hazel's mom had her eyes closed, resting on the couch.

"The news is not good. They picked up the man who threw the ransom note through our window, and they have arrested him. The bad news is, after he got home from our house last night, both his dog and Dot were missing from the doghouse."

"How in the world did they go missing? And a doghouse, in these temperatures?" Hazel questioned. "Why would he leave our dog, or his dog, outside on a cold night? That just seems very mean."

"I agree, Hazel. Not everyone treats their pets as family members and let them in their homes like we do. I don't know if it's a cultural thing or just ignorance."

Boris thought about not being allowed in his warm comfy home and it made him freak out a bit. He jumped off the table and curled up on Hazel's lap. One reason was to make himself feel better, and another was to try to ease some of Hazel's sadness.

Hazel pet Boris's head, fresh tears spilled out of her eyes, slide down her face, and landed on Boris's head. Trying to maintain hope for Dot was getting harder. Hazel's mom rolled over on her side, she looked at Hazel and blew her a kiss.

Wiping her tears away, Hazel kissed Boris on top of his head, then gave her mom a tiny sad smile.

Boris purred and wished he could let Hazel know about all the owls and the crows, who all acted as if Dot was safe.

78 * The Critters * Sunset

The sun dropped below the hills and the trees became silhouetted against the dark blue sky, creating a two-dimensional work of art; it was one of Lily's favorite times of day. All the critters had eaten their dinners and they were restless to get going with the night's mission.

After Lily announced her excitement about joining the mission, Rory's mind started going in overdrive again. "Should we get Bigfoot to help us tonight?", asked Rory. "I mean, what if the coyotes attack us? What if we fall off a cliff? What if a tree falls on someone? What if you trip on a root and hurt your big foot? I think we really need Squatch."

"Caw", said Ruth, who was getting irritated because she was trying to sleep.

Lily giggled, "Rory, you need to stop worrying and you also need to stop eating all of those acorns."

Rory looked at the acorns in his paws, shocked because he didn't even realize he had been eating. "I can't help it. I try, but I just can't stop thinking. It is truly a gift."

This time it was Jojo, who let out a squawk, but it really sounded like a laugh.

"Are you laughing at me?", Rory called to Jojo.

Trying not to laugh again, Jojo said, "No, that was just a pre-sleep snore", as he swayed his head to his soft nighttime beat.

"Okay, everyone, we need let the day birds sleep and get Dot home as quickly as we can.", Lily asserted.

"I will hold down the fort, Lily, and I will be excited to hear from the Broadcasters", hooted Gretchen, the great horned owl.

All the sleepy squirrels squeaked goodbyes and the daytime birds chirped, cawed, and tweeted their farewells, too. There was a hint of sadness in the chatter, they had grown fond of Dot: she was going to be missed.

Lily took a deep breath of the crisp, cold air, getting up her nerve to be a part of the mission. This would be the first time she left the command center on any mission. She felt a mix of excitement and nervous energy. She looked around at all the eyes reflecting at her and grinned at what a sight it was. Foxes, raccoons, dogs, owls, a skunk, and the flying squirrels darting above, back, and forth, between the different trees. It was a great parade line-up.

"Let's do it!", Lily said as they all stepped into the woods.

Gretchen let out a chain of musical hoots to the parade of critters, as they disappeared into the dark woods.

79 * The Night Critters *
Top of The Hill

Lily had a secret, really a backup plan, and the only one that knew her secret was Ester. It was Lily's hope that Ester would be the only one who would ever know it, and that they would not need the backup plan.

The crew had all quieted down after they got into a rhythm of walking through the darkness to the top of the hill. As they looked down, they could see the lights of the town sparkling. Everyone stopped to rest for a moment and take in the sight.

"Getting close.", Lily said to Dot, who looked up to her and wiggled the whole back half of her body. Betty, too, was excited, and let out a very soft howl.

"Down at the bottom of the hill are the railroad tracks, and that is where we will part.", Lily reminded Dot. She sat down so Dot could get in her lap, since the temperature was dropping quickly. Betty wanted some attention, too, so she leaned her whole body against Lily.

That is when Lily saw something out of the corner of her eye. She turned to look, but whatever had been there was gone. Then she saw movement again, but in a different direction.

Lily let out a small whistle to alert Ester. The nimble screech owl started to fly around and use her sharp night vision to check out the surrounding woods.

Ester gave out a low, haunting call to Lily.

Lily returned with a louder whistle to Ester signaling the backup plan.

Ester disappeared through the trees and was gone.

Lily stood up, holding Dot in her arms. Dot could feel the tension in Lily's movement.

"I need you all to come to me, quickly."

The flying squirrels flew down and landed on Lily and the rest of the crew; Morgan, and his six furry youngsters, circled Lily; Funk the skunk ran right next to Abby; the Broadcasters flew to the nearest trees; Rusty and Rose edged closer, too.

"Oh, my. Oh, my, my, my.", Rory was mumbling, as he joined the group. "You are scaring me, Lily. Is it ..."; Lily cut Rory off. She did not have time for his questions.

"The new pack of coyotes have surrounded us."

"How do you know? I don't understand." Rory started up again.

"No more questions. I need everyone that can climb trees to do so right now."

The second she said this, the coyotes started to come out from the shadows. Lily let out a deep roar. Her friends were shocked, because they had only heard kind words and silly giggles from her before.

"Go", Lily demanded.

The flying squirrels and raccoons rushed to the nearest trees. One coyote almost got a flying squirrel, but Abby punched the coyote in the nose. The coyote growled at Abby bearing his shape teeth and started to lunge. Rushing up behind the coyote, Morgan, and Rory each grabbed ahold of the coyote's rear legs. Rory got

133

the left leg and Morgan got the right one, then they both bit down on the back of the coyote's ankles. The coyote let out a yelp and tried to run away but instead hobbled to his pack. Rory and Morgan gave each other a paw bump once they climbed the closest tree.

Lily picked up a hefty stick. A coyote started running directly toward Rose, when Funk the skunk turned around and sprayed the coyote right in its face. The coyote gasped for air and crawled away.

The largest coyote, along with five other coyotes, formed a circle, tightening around the critters on the ground. The raccoons started throwing pinecones at the coyotes, but that didn't deter the coyotes at all. The flying squirrels were also looking for things to drop on the coyotes, but they were caught empty-handed, since it was a surprise attack. Betty, Rusty, and Rose were all growling and baring their teeth, and Funk was trying to reserve the rest of his spray for just the right moment. The Broadcasters started flying down and using their talons to grab the coyotes' tails for a split second, then flying away.

The six coyotes picked up their pace circling as a synchronized unit, full of determination. The closer the coyotes came, the tighter Lily held Dot with her left arm, and the higher she raised her stick with her right arm. Dot locked eyes with the biggest coyote, who seemed to be in a trance staring at her. This scared Dot to her core, and she started shaking but this time it wasn't due to the cold.

80 * The Critters *
Dreams Do Come True

Ester flew up and let out a quick call. Dot could feel Lily relax slightly since Lily's grip loosened. None of the coyotes saw what was coming. In a flash, out stepped Bigfoot; he rushed the largest coyote and lifted it by the tail, until it was dangling down with its head about a foot off the ground. Bigfoot grabbed two more, with his other massive hand. The rest of the coyotes bolted away as fast as they could.

"Great to see you, cuz.", Bigfoot smiled at Lily. "Great to see you, too!" Lily giggled. "Say hey to my friends."

"Hey, y'all." Bigfoot bellowed.

At that moment, they heard a loud crash, and Lily started laughing. She set Dot down and rushed over to pick up Rory. He had fainted, falling off of the tree branch he had been standing on. Lily softly patting his head.

The three remaining coyotes were still dangling from Bigfoot's firm grip, two in one hand and the alpha in the other. Holding the coyotes, higher, Bigfoot looked at them and asked, "Okay, you nasty nitwits, do I have your attention?"

The coyotes each let out a timid yelp.

"If I put you down, you will go, right? I mean gone. Bye-bye. Never see you again. You and the rest of your pack need to move out of our territory. Got it?"

Again, they each let out a yelp.

Bigfoot dropped them on their snouts, roaring, "We would have welcomed you if y'all had been nice!".

The trio took off like their tails were on fire.

Everyone started cheering, and the noise stirred something in Rory's head. Rory opened his eyes, shocked that Lily was holding him.

He wailed, "Why are you holding me like a baby? What is going on here?" Then, he remembered.

"Bigfoot! Oh, Squatchy! I have always dreamed of meeting you, but I never thought I would!", said Rory excitedly, as he jumped out of Lily's arms, ran to Bigfoot hugging the big hairy leg as tight as he could.

Everyone cracked up with relief and joy, after the fright with the coyotes.

Lily cut Rory off, "Cousin, thanks so much for helping. I know we could have handled it, but I thought it would be nice to have you close by just in case the coyotes decide to attack.
Plus, I thought it would be a nice surprise for Rory to see you in action.". She giggled as she looked down at Rory, still glued to Bigfoot's leg.

The raccoons climbed down from the trees and the flying squirrels glided down, landing on their friends.

"Well, like I said earlier, I have missed you. We need to get together more often", said Bigfoot.

"Yes, yes, yes!", Rory shouted.

Lily laughed again, "Okay, Rory, let him go. It would be wonderful to see each other more. We really do need to get going before the temperatures drop, even more."

"Alrighty, it was nice meeting you all and I hope to see you soon.", Bigfoot said, waving as he strode away leaving his big footprints in his wake.

The crew said 'bye' back to him.

Rory chased after Bigfoot, until Lily called him back. Reluctantly, he returned. Standing on his two hind legs, he fell back on soft leaf litter, rejoicing, "Dreams do come true!".

81 * The Critters * Railroad Tracks

"Dot, it has been such a pleasure to have met you. Betty, so nice meeting you too. You have such a warm heart."

Betty did a figure eight through Lily's legs in a playful manner.

"Normally, I never meet the people or animals we help, so this has been wonderful. We hope to see you from afar on the trail with your family in the future; but you must never, ever, run away, again. As you can see, it is safer for you to stay with your humans.", Lily said fondly.

Continuing, "Now that we are on the edge of town, only two land critters are going to go with you. A larger group might attract attention, and we are trying to get you home safely, without any humans noticing. The Broadcasters know the way to your house, so they are going to lead Betty, Rory, Rusty, and you to your home. You all must be careful of cars and getting picked up again, so stay in the shadows, and be safe."

It was sad saying goodbyes to so many friends, although Dot was so excited to be going home, and to feel safe again, but she also knew this was going to be possibly the greatest adventure in her life. It was a bittersweet moment.

Lily leaned down to pick up Dot one last time and gave her a hug. As Lily put Dot down, she reached down to pet Betty.

"I love your big floppy ears! I hope things work out for you, my friend, and I hope you, too, stay safe", Lily gave Betty's ears a tousle with her big hairy hands.

"Y'all need to go. The snow will start to fall any minute now.", Lily warned.

"What do we do if someone sees us? What if someone tries to pick up Betty or Dot? What if"; Lily cut Rory off again.

"You all are going to do great. You got this. Now, go!" Lily ordered.

"What if ….", Rory continued, ignoring Lily.

Lily stopped him again and said, "Go!"

At that moment, the Broadcasters swooped down and circled everyone. Another round of bittersweet goodbyes were quickly said. Lily and her remaining crew headed back to her den, quickly, before Rory could start to ask any more questions.

82 * The Broadcasters *
Leading the Way Home

There were three Broadcasters assigned to the group of critters on the last leg of Dot's journey home. One of the barn owls was keeping an eye out for cars and humans. One was flying a short distance ahead of them, so Dot and crew could follow its lead. The third one was flying to update Barney, at Dot's house, and then Gretchen, at Lily's den.

Ester was there, too, mainly, to help if anything went wrong.

The temperature had been dropping all day and the Arctic wind was getting gutsier by the minute. The blizzard was close.

Luckily, they didn't have far to go, and the barn owls planned a route, believing it was the best path to get Dot home. They avoided most roads and cut through family's yards. After the group of four had crossed over the railroad tracks, they entered the parking lot by the pharmacy. They quickly ran through the parking lot until they got to the alley, where they stopped briefly to make sure the coast was clear. The first big street they had to cross was Main Street. As they crept through the alley toward Main Street, they stayed close to the wall, to remain hidden in the shadows. They waited until they received a cue from the barn owl, that it was safe to cross over the four lanes of Main Street.

After three cars passed by, there was

silence, then they got the hoot to scoot. They all crept out onto the sidewalk. Confirming for themselves that the coast clear and no cars were coming, they bolted across the four lanes. The leading Broadcaster glided into the alley directly across street, by the camping store for them to follow. After passing through the alley, they ran through the parking lot behind the camping store, into the city park.

When Dot was running her body stayed warm, but whenever they stopped to wait, her feet and the tips of her ears felt frozen. So, she was super happy to see the park where they could run, following the fence line by the baseball fields and the dog park.

Rory was trying hard to keep pace with Rusty, Dot, and Betty. He was becoming so winded; he couldn't even think of any questions to ask. There was a lack of oxygen, for sure.

Ester flew down to check in on Rory who was starting to stumble, "You okay?"

Rory held up one of his paws to signal to her he needed to catch his breath.

"Maybe one too many earthworms. Maybe too many nuts, or maybe", Rory gasped.

Ester cut him off, "Okay, why don't you stay here and let Rusty and the Broadcasters get Dot home."

"Oh, I would hate that", Rory complained, but he started to lay down the second, she suggested it.

"It is okay, time is of the essence", said Ester.

The three others had stopped, waiting for Rory to catch up. Dot was anxious to run again. Ester flew down to them, "Rory is going to stay here so you all can get to Dot's home faster."

Dot ran back to Rory and gave him a big lick in the face. Betty followed Dot's lead. Unfortunately, for Rory, Betty had a ton of slobber and soon his face was dripping with all her drool.

"Thanks for the memories", Rory said sarcastically, as he wiped the slobber off.

Both dogs gave a quick bark goodbye and took off after Rusty and the Broadcasters.

"We will see you shortly Rory, get some rest for the trip back to the den.", Ester said.

83 * Home Sweet Home *

Cutting through several yards, triggering motion sensor lights, and having a handful of dogs barking at the small convoy, it was a smooth trip.

Dot froze the moment she saw her house on the other side of the street. Then she saw a new big brown owl flying down by the bay window then back up into the oak tree. Ester flew up and landed right next to this other owl.

Rusty, the fox of very few words, looked at Dot and said, "You ready?"

Dot didn't even reply. Seeing there were no cars, she ran all the way to the front door and started barking like mad.

84 * Boris and The Humans *

Sleeping on the table by the bay window, Boris first thought he was dreaming. He shook his head to get the barking dream to stop. Opening his eyes, he realized it couldn't be a dream because the barking continued. Boris saw Dot outside, and his heart leaped with relief.

Boris let out a huge meow. He tilted his head to hear if there was any movement upstairs. Nope, none.

Hearing Boris meow encouraged Dot to bark louder and faster.

Boris ran up the stairs and jumped on Hazel. The problem was, Hazel slept like a log. Boris went right up to Hazel's ear and let out the loudest, piercing, cat cry he could muster.

Hazel jolted awake, then looked at Boris, totally shocked. Hazel was looking at Boris with wide eyes when she heard Dot barking. She flew out of her bed, threw open the window, and saw two dogs by the front door.

Flying into the hallway, turning on every single light she could, she ran into her parents' room, turning on their lights, all the while screaming, "Dot is home! Dot is home! Dot is home!"

Hazel flew to the twin's room, turning on their lights, chanting, "Dot is home!"

She flew downstairs and jerked the front door open. As Hazel was reaching down to pick Dot, Dot was leaping into Hazel's arms. They twirled around then collapsed in the foyer. The pair rolled around together, with a mixture of tears, laughter, kisses, and tight hugs.

The Colonel stood by the couch with his wife as they both watched this reunion, not wanting to interfere. Finally, feeling the cold air poring through the open door, he treaded lightly to the door. He was about to close the door when he saw Betty.

Betty was sitting there calmly looking up at him. "Come on in.", he told Betty. She was grateful to enter this nice warm home with many wonderful smells.

Before he closed the door, while petting Betty's head, the Colonel announced, "It's snowing! Boy, the flakes are huge."

It was as if Mother Nature had waited until Dot got inside before she let the snow fall.

Hearing the Colonel, and before he had closed the door, Dot looked out the door to try to see if she could see Rusty or one of the owls. But she didn't see any of them. This hurt her a bit, because she would've loved to have said thank you and goodbye to her friends. What Dot didn't know was that the owls were watching through the bay window, and Rusty was honored that he got to witness the reunion through the open door, from across the street. With a warm heart, Rusty went to go find Rory, so they could get home before too much snow fell.

The twins slowly made their way down the stairs in their sleepy stupor. Hazel's mom and the Colonel joined Hazel on the floor to greet Dot with lots of hugs and kisses, too. Betty was sitting down and smiling, as she watched everyone.

It was a gorgeous moment, a top ten, for sure.

85 * The Broadcasters *

The Broadcasters and Ester were soaring high with joy, excited to share the news. First, they reported it to Gretchen, who was outside Lily's den. Gretchen could hardly wait to tell all the critters and Lily, in the morning, about the successful reunion. But she didn't want to wake them now because they were all sound asleep in the den, exhausted from the mission.

The Broadcasters then flew to the moonshine man's shack to let the owl stationed there know. That owl would then tell Opal, the possum, and the crow, when they woke up in the morning. Benny the bear would hear about the successful reunion whenever he woke up from hibernation. The good news would be shared with all who had helped make this mission successful, including the river otters and Beverly the beaver. Everyone, that is, except the Canada geese, because who knows where they are. Somewhere south, maybe Georgia, Florida, Alabama ... who knows.

86 * Hazel & Furry Friends * Pre-Breakfast

Hazel woke up and smiled, her bed was full with two dogs and one big orange cat. Dot was sound asleep right next to her under the covers tucked by her legs. Hazel tried to nudge Dot awake, but Dot was out like a sack of potatoes. Boris, who had never slept in Hazel's bed with Dot, was sound asleep, almost completely on top of Dot, but above the covers.

Hazel had always wanted her two animals to get along and it saddened her Boris had been so jealous of Dot. Seeing them so close now, warmed her heart and tears of gratitude rolled down her cheek. To be honest, the tears were also from relief and happiness that her best friend was home. She had feared this day would never come.

The only one awake was Betty, who was curled up at Hazel's feet watching Hazel's every move, all the while taking deep sniffs of the frying bacon downstairs. Hazel looked at Betty's deep black droopy eyes and her huge floppy ears. Hazel loved seeing her lying in the thickness of the big blankets on her warm bed, instead of thinking about Betty being outside in her doghouse, chained up on this cold, snowy morning.

That thought alone made Hazel shudder. "I am sure you miss your owner, but you are welcome here until he gets out of jail. I'll tell you one thing, he and I are going to have a talk, and he will need to agree to a few things before I let him have you back." Betty looked at Hazel; it seemed Betty understood, Hazel thought. What Hazel didn't know was that Betty did understand, and she whole heartedly agreed.

With that, Hazel announced, "Good morning, everyone. Let's go downstairs and get us some delicious bacon." Boris let out a mixture of a yawn and a meow and Betty let out a small woof, but Dot was still sound asleep. Hazel pulled the 'sack of potatoes' on her lap and whispered in her ear, "Bacon, bacon, bacon."

Slowly, Dot opened her eyes, then she rolled off Hazel's lap onto her back with her legs sticking right up to the ceiling and began her morning routine, which the family called 'Dot's morning wiggles".

Hazel laughed, leaned down to kiss Boris, then Dot, she jumped off the bed, and she hugged Betty's neck. Hazel marched quite proudly as she went down the stairs, followed by the parade of all her furry friends to the wonderful smells of the kitchen.

87 * Jail *
Lunchtime

Jimbo was just finishing his lunch of ham, collard greens, and some buttery corn bread that Deputy Peter had brought him from his home. "I have to tell ya, Peter, that was some of the best

146

home cooking I have had in a long time. Not much of a cooker myself. I guess that is why I am so skinny. Ha.", the moonshine man chuckled.

He was in a small jail cell right next to the Deputy's desk. The cell was normally empty, since the town was so small and peaceful.

"You sure do need some meat on them there bones, that's for sure", Peter laughed at Jimbo. "But I wouldn't suggest that you ever get as big as me", as he rubbed his round belly.

"Jimbo, I am going to get a bit serious. I feel so guilty because I knew you had to be lonely, and I didn't do anything about it. I guess I got busy with family, raising three boys with football, baseball, and goodness knows what. Every time I saw you driving around town, I meant to reach out to you, but I never did. I feel awful about that. That being said, I was so surprised that you did what you did. The only law your family ever broke was selling moonshine; other than that, you all were super law abiding.", Peter sighed. "I've talked with the sheriff, and I told him I wanted to work with you. Bring you into the fold of our family and help you out. I know, in my heart, if you hadn't lost your brothers and your pa, you would've never done what you did."

Jimbo looked at Peter through the bars of the jail cell, tears were streaming down his cheeks. He pulled an old faded red bandanna out of the front pocket of his threadbare overalls, wiping away his tears and nodding his head.

Peter continued, "The sheriff is from a big town, and he is not quite sure about all of this. I assured him that, if we talk with the family of the dog and they agree, we can work out a deal. But you will still have to do community service. I'm taking a lot of responsibility here, but I think I can trust you. You agree, don't ya, Jimbo?"

Jimbo nodded, but what he was really feeling was a great sense of sadness melt away. The thought of having something of a family again was overwhelming. Some of his favorite memories were of playing in the school yard with his brothers, Peter, and Peter's brothers.

"There was one thing the sheriff wouldn't agree to, and that was us turning a blind eye on you selling moonshine, so that will have to stop. So, as a family, we will figure out some law-abiding way for you to make money."

"Thank you, Peter.", was all the moonshine man could manage to say, as his tears continued to flow. It was so nice to have someone to care for him again.

88 * All the Humans at Dot's Home *

Hazel's parents, the sheriff, Peter, and Jimbo were all sitting down in the living room, talking. Peter had just updated the parents on all the history that had led Jimbo to take Dot and, hopefully, some of the future, if the family agreed. Hazel came in the front door, with Dot and Betty on leashes.

"What is going on here?", she demanded, as she unhooked the dogs. "You are the man that took my dog. Why would you do that? I also heard that your dog sleeps in a doghouse, even in the winter. That is just cruel. Dogs get cold just like us. They feel the weather too, both hot and cold. Plus, they have feelings just like us. Have you ever seen a happy dog compared to a sad dog?"

"Hazel.", the Colonel said, "Let's be polite."

"I just want to know.", Hazel continued.

"Uh, uh, uh.", was all that Jimbo could muster. He had never seen a kid be this demanding to an adult; it was kind of shocking. Had he acted like that, his grandma would have let him have it.

"Jimbo?", Peter said, knowing full well what Jimbo was thinking. He, too, thought these younger kids were very outspoken.

"Uh, uh, I was just following what my daddy did, what his daddy did, and his daddy's daddy did.", Jimbo stuttered out.

"Hazel, the deputy here has asked us to consider not to press charges. It is a long story, and we will tell you later, but he is asking us if there are any special requests we might make if we don't press charges."

"Oh, I have a list", Hazel piped. The Colonel knew how his daughter felt about animals, so he knew it was best for them to step away.

"Please excuse us while we discuss this in a different room.", the Colonel said.

"No problem", the sheriff agreed.

Feeling some of the tension leave the room, Betty finally felt it was okay to go to her owner. Jimbo looked at his red girl and, as he petted her, he thought about everything Hazel had said.

"My daddy always said dogs didn't have feelings, but I used to feel the same way as that little girl did, when I was a boy", Jimbo said softly.

"I hated the dogs sleeping outside, but then I just followed my daddy's ways. I wonder why I did that?"

"I guess we were trained, just like a dog, to follow old rules. Or you could say you can't teach an old dog new tricks.", Peter reply, trying to lighten the mood.

Minutes later, the parents and Hazel came out to join the three men. The Colonel said, "Well, we understand that you really aren't that mean, but very grumpy because of life throwing a bunch of lemons at you. I know life can be tough sometimes. I too, lost both my parents at a young age. But luckily, I had a wonderful uncle that raised me", he reflected to Jimbo.

Jimbo looked at the Colonel in a new light. He had been jealous of this man, but to think that he, too, felt the pain of losing both of his parents, made him feel a connection with him.

"Hazel has a list of demands, and my wife and I agree with her. We would like for you to share your home with Betty, so that she is safe from bugs, coyotes, rain, snow, and the summer heat. We also think Betty is too skinny, so we would like you to give her a bit more, and better quality, food. Hazel would also like to have Betty come to our house for weekly visits, since she feels strongly that your dog and Dot have become very close. That's, it. That is all we want.", the Colonel said.

All eyes then looked at Dot and Betty, who were both curled up on the sofa together, sound asleep, still tired from their journey.

Jimbo looked at Peter and the sheriff, "I can agree with all that. Maybe one day I can even afford a fancy pillow I see some dogs have."

Hazel smiled, "That would be very nice of you." The sheriff stood up, "I think we have a fine agreement. Jimbo, as part of your community service I would like to work with you and Betty here, to train her so if anyone ever gets lost in the woods, you two can help us find them. Maybe, one day, it could be a part time job for you."

Jimbo nodded humbly and everyone else smiled, as the tension in the room finally evaporated. Even Boris could feel the shift and let out a big meow.

The End

Please Follow Lily On Socail Media

 YouTube-Shesquatch

 TiTok- @shesquatchlives

Instagram -
@Shesquiatch_she_exists

 Facebook - Shesquatch

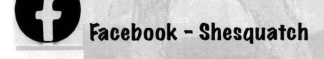 Twitter-@Shesquatchlives

OTHER PUBLICATIONS BY
SALLY W EPPSTEIN

Available @ www.shesquatch.org
Also @ Amazon.com

MEET LILY
A SHESQUATCH

WRITTEN AND ILLUSTRATED BY SALLY W EPPSTEIN

Made in the USA
Columbia, SC
07 December 2022

72921313R00098